EXCITEMENT, SUSPENSE—AND
KAY TRACEY—GO TOGETHER!

Sixteen-year-old Kay Tracey is an amateur detective with a sense of sleuthing that a professional might envy. Her closest friends who share her adventures are Betty Worth and her twin sister Wendy. Whenever there is a mystery in the small town of Brantwood, you'll find Kay and her two friends in the middle of it.

If you like spine-tingling action and heart-stopping suspense, follow the trail of Kay and her friends in the other books in this series: *The Double Disguise, In the Sunken Garden, The Six Fingered Glove Mystery, The Green Cameo Mystery* and *The Message in the Sand Dunes.*

A Kay Tracey Mystery

THE MANSION
OF
SECRETS

Frances K. Judd

A BANTAM SKYLARK BOOK

THE MANSION OF SECRETS
A Bantam Skylark Book/published by arrangement with
Lamplight Publishing, Inc.

PRINTING HISTORY

Hardcover edition published in 1978 exclusively by Lamplight
Publishing, Inc.
Bantam Skylark edition/October 1980

ISBN 0-553-15070-7

Published simultaneously in the United States and Canada

PRINTED IN THE UNITED STATES OF AMERICA

0 9 8 7 6 5 4 3 2 1

BOOK DESIGNED BY MIERRE

Contents

The Mansion
of
Secrets

"Gold coins!" Kay exclaimed.

I

The Deserted Mansion

"Here comes the postman," announced Kay Tracey cheerfully.

She got up from the breakfast table and hurried to the front door. Her mother and her cousin, Bill Tracey, a young lawyer, looked up expectantly from their morning coffee as she returned a moment later.

"A nice, fat letter for me, and several for you, Mother," said the girl, sorting a handful of mail. "Nothing but dull looking business letters for Bill," she went on, "though this top one might be interesting. It has a Wyoming postmark." She placed several envelopes by his plate.

Bill laid down his newspaper and read the Wyoming letter as he munched his toast.

"Whew!" he whistled. "This certainly is interesting! A man from Wyoming wants to buy the old Greely place near here. What a load off my mind that is!"

"How are you involved with selling that dreary mansion?" asked Mrs. Tracey.

"You're a lawyer, not a real estate agent," added Kay.

"I'm trying to settle an estate," explained Bill. "After old Manuel Greely died, without a will, I was put in charge by the court. The only heir I could find was a grandnephew, Peter Greely. He asked me to sell the place, if I could."

"I've never heard of any Peter Greely," reflected Mrs. Tracey, who knew almost everyone in the little town of Brantwood.

"Peter's never lived here and isn't planning to now. He had the furniture from the old house put into storage and the place boarded up. He's an airplane pilot, by the way."

"That's exciting," said Kay.

"Who wants to buy the Greely place?" asked Mrs. Tracey.

"Who in the world would want that spooky property?" asked her daughter. "People say it's haunted! There are all sorts of strange stories about it."

"It's four miles out of town among those lonely hills and deep woods," shuddered Mrs. Tracey.

"It's even called 'The Mansion of Secrets,'" added her daughter.

"I wonder why?" her mother mused.

"There's supposed to be a fortune hidden in the house somewhere," explained Kay.

"I'd be glad to be rid of the responsibility of being in charge of it," Bill sighed.

"Why would anyone from Wyoming want to buy that place?" Mrs. Tracey asked.

"He writes that he wants to turn it into a dude ranch. Located here in the East, it will be accessible to more customers than the spot he has in the West, so he can make more money."

"A ranch! That's terrific!" cried Kay.

"He's a young man by the name of Clarence Cody," added Bill Tracey, reading the signature. "He will open it as a resort and riding school."

"It has a good location for that," agreed Mrs. Tracey. "There must be ten miles or more of dense woodland stretching back from the huge estate. Any number of bridle paths could be used for riding parties."

"And those enormous stables and pastures could easily accommodate the horses," added Bill.

"I think it'll be a lot of fun," Kay said enthusiastically.

"You'd better hurry, dear, or you'll be late for school," warned Mrs. Tracey suddenly.

"I'm on my way," Kay answered as she gathered up her books. "Oh, Cousin Bill, can I have a key to the Greely house so that after school some of us can go out and explore Mystery Manor? I've always wanted to, and if the place is going to be sold soon this will be my last chance."

"I suppose so," agreed her cousin, fumbling in his pocket for a key ring. "I'll lend you the rear entrance key and keep the one to the front door for myself. If you and your friends can run out there this afternoon and take the 'For Sale' sign off the house it will save me a trip."

"Perhaps we'll find the hidden fortune!" said Kay, her brown eyes sparkling.

"You won't find anything but dust and broken glass, I'm afraid," laughed the attorney.

"I can hardly wait!" cried Kay.

Giving her mother a quick kiss she left the house and hurried downtown. Kay was a slender, attractive girl in her teens, with alert brown eyes and light curly brown hair that reflected copper glints in the sunshine. At the railroad station she joined a group of students who traveled back and forth daily to the high school in the nearby town of Carmont.

"You almost missed the train, Kay," called Wendy Worth, a dark, studious girl.

"What made you late? Here's the train," added Wendy's sister Betty.

Although Betty and Wendy were twins they were not at all alike. Betty was as blonde as Wendy was dark and as lighthearted as Wendy was serious. They were Kay's closest friends.

"Wait till you hear the latest news!" Kay said as the three climbed aboard the train.

"You're not up to something new!" protested Betty in mock despair as they found seats. "Kay, you *do* get into the most exciting adventures."

Kay laughed. As the train sped along she explained about the old house, its airplane pilot heir, and the man from Wyoming who planned to turn the Greely estate into a dude ranch.

"Best of all," Kay concluded, "my cousin Bill said we can explore the Mansion of Secrets this afternoon!"

To this Wendy poetically recited:

"They say 'Coming events cast their shadows before them,'
And the gloom of that mansion bare
Makes me feel in my bones that trouble will come,
So I warn you, beware, and take care!"

"There you go being gloomy again," said Betty impatiently. "We'd never have adventures if we listened to your warnings!"

"Wendy is poetic and more sensitive than we are," said Kay with a smile.

"Here we are at Carmont," broke in Betty. "How I'll be able to sit through school with an adventure brewing, I don't know!"

Although Kay partially agreed with Betty, she was

more interested in her classes than her friend was. Her chemistry teacher, Doctor Staunton, had helped her out of a difficulty in her last mystery, and she worked hard on his class assignments. He announced on this particular morning that in a few days he would take a group of students to a perfume factory for a special lecture on how the rare oils were obtained.

"It'll be a sweet trip," giggled Betty when she and Wendy met Kay after school. "Well, let's hurry so we can get to the Greely place before dark."

Since the mansion lay four miles outside of Brantwood, Kay suggested that they go to her house, get the Tracey car, and drive there. During the ride the girls exchanged stories about the place and speculated on what secrets it might hold. Finally Kay turned the car from the smooth state highway onto a rough dirt road. This went past the deserted estate, which was about half a mile farther on.

"Someone else seems to be going there, too," Kay remarked as she neared a dusty green car ahead. "It's a woman."

"Slow down and let her reach the place first," urged Betty. "Then, if she goes in we'll follow her and find out what she wants."

Kay slowed her car and the green car shot ahead. Sure enough, it turned into the winding driveway that led between rows of dark, drooping hemlock trees into the spacious grounds of the Greely estate. The big house itself stood on the crest of a little hill overlooking a vast expanse of woods. The green car came to a stop in front of it, and the unknown visitor went up the steps, unlocked the great front door, and walked in!

"She acts as if she belongs here!" marvelled Betty.

"Cousin Bill says lots of people prowl around this place but no one except Peter Greely has any legal right to," said Kay, stepping from the automobile some distance away from the house. "Let's walk to the mansion without that woman seeing us."

The three friends hurried on foot along the hemlock-shaded drive. Ahead of them was the immense rambling house with porches, balconies and towers. Its three stories above the basement rose high amid the tall, dismal fir trees that shielded it.

"It looks like a cardboard model I've seen of a castle," commented Wendy. "I love the little glass turret on top of the roof!"

"There must be a great view of the countryside from that lookout," Kay answered.

The mansion, which at one time had been painted a forbidding battleship gray, had faded until now it was as pale as fog.

"I have a key to the kitchen entrance," Kay explained. "Quick, come this way!"

Followed by the twins, Kay scuttled hastily to the door, which opened after a heavy push. The friends found themselves in an enormous old-fashioned kitchen.

"Listen!" cautioned Betty. "That woman is in the front hall. I can hear her."

Stepping as softly as cats over the creaky boards, the friends found themselves in a butler's pantry off the kitchen. Through a crack in the door they could peek into the lofty main hallway.

A majestic staircase rose in a graceful spiral to the floor above. At the foot of this stairway the strange intruder was stooping over, feeling the steps with her hands.

"She must have dropped something," Wendy whispered.

The dumpy little woman, of middle age, was neatly but plainly dressed. She carried a black shopping bag which she now opened.

"She has tools in it!" gasped Betty.

To the surprise of the watchers in the pantry, the smug little woman took out a chisel and a hammer! She carefully counted the steps from the bottom, then suddenly began to tap on one of them.

"It's the seventh," Kay observed.

Appearing satisfied with her choice, the woman next forced the sharp edge of her chisel under the tread and whacked it in violently with her hammer. Finally she pushed up hard on the tool handle. There was a screech of loosened nails and the board yawned open. The treasure seeker peered into the hollow and gave a little cry.

"She found something," murmured Kay.

"Let me see!" begged Betty, pushing closer.

In her excitement Betty moved too quickly, tripped over Wendy's feet, and fell sprawling. Her head hit the pantry door with a bang!

Instantly the fortune hunter sprang up, startled by the noise. She let her tools fall with a clatter and scurried quickly down a passageway.

"Let's catch her!" shouted Kay.

II

The New Heir

_____

"She's disappeared!" cried Betty in disappointment as the three girls started in pursuit of the woman.

"Quick, this way!" Kay called, racing along another passageway. "Oh, no, it's a dead end!" she said, then stopped short.

She had come to the door of a small room that must have been a den or study. It was empty of furniture, but some old, faded prints still hung on the dusty walls.

"Don't leave me behind!" Wendy cried, hurrying into the room with the others.

"Listen!" cautioned Kay, cocking her head and listening intently. "A motor! The woman's leaving!"

Quickly the girls scrambled to an unboarded window and peered out.

"There she goes," mourned Betty, as the green car bounced wildly over the rough road under the hemlocks.

"I'd like to know if she found anything," mused Wendy.

"I wonder how she knew where to look," puzzled Kay.

"There must be something in these stories of hidden treasure after all," Betty remarked. "Let's look for secret hiding places ourselves."

"Well, if there *is* anything here, it should be turned

over to Peter Greely before the property is sold," murmured Kay.

"Where would you begin to look?" asked Wendy hopelessly. "It's such a huge house. We can't go tapping stairs and walls at random and expect to find something."

"True," agreed Kay. "I think that woman must have inside information."

"She sure went right to the spot and knew exactly what to do," Betty assented.

"Let's look at that seventh step," suggested Kay, turning back toward the main hall.

"We're lost in another passageway!" cried Wendy in dismay.

"I never saw such a place!" exclaimed Betty irritably. "It's an impossible maze of narrow halls, little unexpected rooms, doors leading into huge dark closets—"

"And one room leading into another, endlessly—" added her sister, poking her head through a doorway.

"Look!" cried Kay. "An old elevator shaft to complicate things even more!"

The empty opening rose dark and drafty at one end of the main hall. Betty slammed its door, remarking, "A great place for ghosts or tramps! It gives me the creeps!"

"Old Mr. Greely must have had heart trouble and had to ride up and down stairs," Kay decided.

"Well, he had too many nooks and crannies in his home to suit me," said Betty, looking uneasily over her shoulder.

"You half expect to see a ghost suddenly step out of a doorway," added Wendy in a whisper. She had hardly spoken when heavy footsteps resounded on the front porch and somebody rattled the doorknob! "Who's that?" she gasped.

The enormous panelled front door swung open and then banged shut, the sound echoing through the empty rooms like the roar of a cannon. The twins held back but Kay looked out to see who the newcomer was.

"It's a man, and he's very good looking!" she reported.

The young man, whoever he was, entered whistling, and marched down the big front hall. He made no effort to be quiet and his footsteps resounded on the bare floors as he strode toward the den.

"Bill said people prowl around here constantly," whispered Kay, "but I had no idea they came this often."

"Almost a traffic problem," Betty snickered.

Wendy clapped a hand over her sister's mouth to muffle her laughter, and added a sharp "Sh!"

"This man acts like he belongs here. Let's see what he's looking for," Kay suggested.

She led the way down the passage to the den. The twins tiptoed after her. Guided by the man's cheerful whistle and echoing footsteps, the three girls reached the small study and peered in. The intruder turned and saw them.

"Well, well, hello there!" the man greeted them pleasantly. "What are you young ladies doing here, may I ask?"

"What are *you* doing here?" returned Kay.

"I'm just taking these old prints," he answered casually, and went on removing the faded pictures from the walls.

"Have you the right to?" Kay asked.

"They belong to me," replied the young man.

"Then you must be Peter Greely!" exclaimed Kay.

"The same!" said the handsome stranger with a friendly smile. "Now you must introduce yourselves!"

Kay promptly did so, explaining that the attorney

in charge of the Greely estate was her cousin, Bill Tracey. "That's why we're here," she concluded. "Bill asked us to take down the 'For Sale' sign."

"So it's actually sold at last!" reflected Peter Greely. "I wonder who's buying it? I haven't heard about it from Mr. Tracey."

"A man from Wyoming is buying it to use as a riding club and resort, a sort of imitation Western ranch," Kay explained. "I think his name is Clarence Cody."

"Never heard of him but I wish him luck in his project," laughed Peter.

"Have you ever heard any story about there being a fortune hidden in the house somewhere?" asked Kay. "You might find that, and it might be more valuable than the price Mr. Cody would pay for the mansion."

"Yes," Peter Greely laughed. "I've heard those tall tales of hidden valuables, but I'm convinced they're just rumors."

"Have you ever explored the place, or tried to find out if there might be something hidden here?" asked Kay.

"To tell you the truth, I have," Peter admitted. "I'm always hard up and the idea of buried treasure lured me. This legend of a concealed fortune was so tantalizing that I did search for it at one time."

"No luck?" asked Betty.

"No luck whatever," chuckled Peter. "It's all sort of silly, it seems to me. Every empty old mansion acquires the reputation of being haunted or full of hidden secrets of one kind or another. As far as my old uncle's home is concerned, I'm positive the stories are all nonsense and gossip. I'll gladly turn over the gossip with the rest of the property to the enterprising cowboy Cody!"

"Do you mind if we look around a little before Mr.

Cody takes over the place?" asked Kay eagerly.

"Go right ahead and search all you want!" answered Peter. "I hope your efforts will turn up something besides rats' nests and torn wallpaper and fallen plaster! I warn you, though, you'll find you're only wasting your time."

"It'll be fun, anyway," responded Kay.

"Make yourselves at home!" the young heir replied hospitably. "This place has never been a home to me!"

"Do you live near here?" asked Betty, helping to remove a picture from the dingy wall.

"I'm afraid I'm a wanderer; a rolling stone," answered Peter Greely cheerfully. "I never stay long in one place, although I keep Bill Tracey informed of all my forwarding addresses. Right now I'm flying a specially designed airplane to England for that government's approval."

"Oh, how exciting!" cried Wendy.

"Yes, I think it's fun myself. That's why I do it," responded Peter.

"I think flying must be the most wonderful sensation in the world," said Wendy dreamily.

"Look out!" warned the practical Betty. "She's going to burst into poetry any minute now. I can always tell by that faraway look in her eyes. I'm sure you're rhyming fly, high and sky, aren't you, Wendy?" she teased.

Poor Wendy flushed. "Don't you feel like a great hawk or a swift sea gull when you soar over the ocean through the clouds?" she asked the pilot, ignoring Betty's taunt.

"I'm afraid not," said the young man kindly. "I'm not very poetic or romantic. I enjoy flying, but to tell you the truth I don't feel a bit like a bird."

"What do you think about when you are all alone in the sky above the clouds?" persisted Wendy wistfully.

"I generally hope the fuel holds out, or I wish I were on the ground eating a steak and French fried potatoes!"

Wendy's sensitive face clouded. She stood looking at one of the old prints she had taken from a wall. It was the picture of a sea gull with graceful wings spread.

"I will always think of flying as being like this sea bird, the very poetry of motion," she murmured.

"Then you keep the picture and think of it in that beautiful way," answered Peter, as if to make up for having disappointed her.

"Oh, I couldn't take this. It's too pretty and it belongs to you," Wendy protested.

"Since it is mine, I can give it away!" insisted Peter. "In fact, I'd be happy if each of you would pick out any of these prints you like. I don't want them and I have no place to put them except in storage with the furniture."

"Oh, they're much too valuable for you to give away!" objected Betty.

"You could sell them. They're beautiful!" added Kay.

"I think they're dirty and unattractive," laughed Peter Greely, "and I don't want to be bothered with them!"

Finally persuaded, Kay decided on a picture of a bright humming bird poised over a spray of flowers. Betty chose a vivid sprig of blossoms.

"Keep them to remember me by while I'm above the clouds," laughed the pilot, and with a cheerful good-bye he strode away, his few remaining pictures tucked carelessly under one arm.

"What an amazing person!" said Wendy.

"He sure is! And now that we have his permission to pry about, treasure hunting, let's start right now," urged Kay.

"But where do we start?"

"On the steps, of course," replied Kay.

She returned to the stairway and picked up the chisel and hammer which had been dropped there.

"I suppose you are going to start tapping like a woodpecker," said Betty.

"Personally I never can tell," declared Wendy, "whether a watermelon is ripe or not by thumping it. I'm sure I couldn't tell whether a step had a treasure in it or not just by knocking on it!"

Undaunted, Kay was examining each step minutely, feeling, tapping and listening. The seventh step was empty!

"If Kay thinks she can unravel a mystery, I know from past experience that she will!" asserted Betty.

"Yes," her sister agreed, "you've given us plenty of adventures, Kay, ever since you began solving one mystery after another."

"Maybe I've begun to unravel this one!" her friend answered suddenly. "This step doesn't sound hollow. Listen, it goes 'plunk, plunk,' as if it were filled with something. Let's pry it open."

"It's the eleventh step," said Betty, counting.

"Sure enough, and I've heard there's luck in the seven-eleven combination," Wendy spoke up. "Open it up, Kay! Hurry!"

III

Hidden Treasure

Wendy and Betty watched intently as Kay Tracey went to work with hammer and chisel to force open the eleventh step. Again there was the harsh screech of nails giving way. Once more a step yawned open. Three pairs of eyes peered hopefully into the hole.

"Nothing but dirty old papers!" Wendy exclaimed, bitterly disappointed.

"Wonder what this is?" said Kay, lifting out a closely rolled bundle of stiff sheets.

"Spread them out, Kay, so we can see what's on them," Betty urged.

Already her friend had blown off some of the dust and was unrolling the sheaf on the hall floor.

"These aren't paper at all," she discovered. "They are some sort of glazed linen with drawings on them in India ink."

"Maps, maybe?" asked Betty, looking over her shoulder.

"Oh, I know what they are!" Wendy cried. "An architect's plan of a house! Don't you remember, Betty? Great-grandfather Worth was an architect and drew plans on that shiny cloth that wouldn't tear. He made some picture scrapbooks for Mom out of the material when she was small. They use blueprints for plans now, but Great-grandfather's drawings were exactly like these!"

"You're right, Wendy. Look here!" Kay cried, pointing to some neat lettering in a lower corner of the top sheet. The twins leaned over and read:

ORIGINAL PLANS FOR DWELLING
of
MANUEL GREELY, ESQUIRE
by
JOHN VINSON, ARCHITECT

"If these drawings had been on plain paper or been blueprints they would have been ruined long ago," remarked Betty, fingering the cloth.

"As it is, they're as good as new," Wendy noted.

"These are the plans for this very house," said Kay, examining them closely. Then she broke into a sudden shout of excitement.

"Oh! Oh! Oh! Look!"

"Look at what?" chorused the twins in bewilderment.

"Don't you see anything important on these sheets?" Kay asked.

"No," said Betty. "I can't make head or tail of them!"

"Don't you see here and there on the plans the little red ink X's with the word IMPORTANT printed after each one?"

"Yes, I see them," Wendy admitted.

"What are they for? To indicate the plumbing?" asked Betty.

"No, no, no!" exclaimed Kay. "Look, here's one marked on the seventh step of the staircase and another on the eleventh. And lots of others."

"Secret hiding places!" Wendy cried.

"I think so," said Kay. "Now all we'll have to do is follow these plans and locate the hidden fortune!"

"I can't believe it will be as simple as that!" disagreed Betty skeptically.

"We can test it," Wendy argued. "Which 'X' shall we go after first, Kay?"

Kay pored over the papers. "Let's try this one," she suggested, pointing. "It indicates the second-floor back hall and appears to be a set of built-in drawers."

"All right," agreed Betty. "Let's go up the rear stairway."

"Good idea," said Kay, leading the way toward the kitchen.

"Hurry up!" implored Betty, stumbling up the steep steps.

"Here we are," said Kay, "and here is the built-in set of drawers at the head of the stairs."

"It seems to be a sort of linen closet," observed Betty, energetically jerking out one drawer after another. "Nothing in any of them," she reported in disgust.

"Let me look," offered Wendy more patiently. Carefully she examined each compartment, and with Kay's help peered in every nook and cranny behind the empty drawers.

"Absolutely nothing," groaned Wendy. "I think the whole thing is a hoax. Peter Greely would know about any family fortune if it really were here! I think he's right, it's all nonsense and a waste of time!"

"I'm afraid so," echoed her sister. "Come on, Kay, we have to start for home. It's getting late."

"And we don't want to be in this spooky place when it gets dark!" shivered Wendy.

"Just let me look once more," pleaded Kay, who was not easily discouraged.

"Make it snappy then," replied Betty.

Wendy and Betty wandered off through the vast empty bedrooms on a little exploring tour of their own, while Kay began another thorough examination of the wall cavity. The hollow behind the first drawer revealed nothing. Back of the second Kay felt only a rusty nail on which she scratched a finger. Reaching into the space behind the third compartment, she was about to give up when, by accident, her hand knocked against a small block of wood. Instantly a tiny panel sprang open!

"Bet-ty! Wen-dy! I've found something!" she called excitedly.

Probing into the niche with eager fingers she pulled out a smooth leather case. Wendy and Betty dashed down the hall just as Kay's thumb pressed a button on it. The lid snapped open and revealed to their astonished gaze *a glitter of diamonds!*

"Fantastic!" exclaimed Betty, her eyes bulging.

"It must be worth a fortune," murmured Wendy breathlessly.

"This diamond stickpin is beautiful!" cried Kay, picking up one of the articles carefully.

"And look at those gorgeous cuff links!" Wendy exclaimed.

"I can hardly believe my eyes!" gasped Betty.

"Here's a diamond-studded belt buckle," said Kay, lifting it gently from the satin-lined jewel case.

"Let's get out of here before more fortune hunters come thumping around trying to claim these valuables," advised Betty.

"Yes, I don't want to stay in this lonely spot at dusk with a fortune in jewels," added Wendy.

"I should tell cousin Bill about this right away," agreed Kay. "This collection legally belongs to Peter Greely."

"I guess our friend the airplane pilot won't want to sell the house now," reflected Betty.

"I guess not!" Kay replied. "Especially since the plans show other marked places which probably hold more valuable things."

"It's lucky you found this before the property was actually sold," Wendy said with a sigh of satisfaction.

"We've got to take down the 'For Sale' sign before we leave," said Kay, clattering down the back stairs, the jewel box in her hand.

Accordingly the announcement on the post at the entrance to the property was torn off. This done, the three treasure seekers raced home as fast as Kay dared to drive. They burst in excitedly upon Mrs. Tracey and Bill, who had begun to eat their dinner.

"Come on, girls, join us," invited Kay's mother.

"We're too excited to eat!" protested Wendy and Betty. "Wait till you see what Kay found in the Mansion of Secrets!"

The lawyer gave a long, shrill whistle when the jewels were spread before him.

"And look at these plans. We've got to go back and check out every one of the spots marked 'X Important,'" said Kay.

After dinner she placed the drawings on the library table under the glow of a lamp. The open jewel case now lay in the bright light also, the diamonds twinkling with fiery red and blue gleams. A breeze from the open window rustled the sheets as the Traceys and the Worth girls bent over, pointing and talking excitedly. So occupied was each of them that nobody noticed a greedy pair of eyes watching them from the darkness outside the library window!

"Tomorrow we'll take these gems to a jeweler to have them appraised," decided Bill. "Then we'll go back and check these clues to see if some more valuables are hidden in the mansion."

Upon hearing this remark the stealthy watcher at the open window slunk away unobserved. It wasn't necessary to wait to hear what would be said by the girls as they sat down to a late dinner. He had heard enough.

"I'm glad tomorrow is Saturday so we can start out on our treasure hunt first thing in the morning," said Betty. "I'd burst if I had to wait until after school!"

"We'll see you in the morning, for sure!" Wendy added as she and her twin left for home.

Early the next day Kay stopped for Wendy and Betty on her way to the jeweler's with her lawyer cousin.

"Won't it be disappointing if those stones turn out to be imitations!" said Wendy pessimistically.

They found that the jewels were by no means imitations. Indeed, the jeweler's evaluation of them was so high that Bill immediately put them into the bank vault.

"And now," Bill announced, "we'll investigate that mysterious property thoroughly! Are you sure that you've got the plans, Kay?"

"Yes!" his cousin replied.

As soon as the search party reached Greely Manor and had entered the great hall, Kay spread the plans on the floor for everyone to examine. Red 'X's peppered the black ink drawings.

"This house is so huge that we'll have to go about this systematically," began Bill.

"Each of us can take a spot marked 'X,' and then we'll cover the ground more quickly," suggested Kay.

"OK, I'll take this secret panel marked on the side wall of the den," Bill volunteered.

"I choose the knob of the newel post on the

second-floor banister," said Kay. "I suppose it un-screws."

"Wendy and I will take that window seat in the second-floor back hallway," decided Betty.

Leaving the plans spread out conveniently on the floor, the fortune hunters hurried off on their adventure. Bill had difficulty locating his panel because the wall long ago had been completely papered over. It covered any sign of a possible opening. Kay discovered that her knob was stuck fast. It refused to budge in spite of her efforts. It was the Worth twins who let out the first shout of triumph.

"We've found something!" they called.

There came a clang and a heavy thud, followed by cries of dismay. Kay and Bill Tracey rushed to the scene.

"I hope I haven't ruined them if they are of any value," Betty was saying.

She had dropped a large metal box and three very old books. Bill carefully picked them up.

"They're Bibles!" he exclaimed in astonishment. "They are so old they must be very valuable. One is dated 1551 and here's another dated 1771. They're priceless!"

"Here is some writing on this heavy wrapping paper that was around them," Kay discovered. She deciphered the faded words which read:

BOOK COLLECTOR'S ITEM: Bible of 1551 called "The Bug Bible" because in the Ninety First Psalm, for the usual line, "Thou shalt not be afraid of any terror by night" it reads, "of any bugges (bogies) by night." The 1771 volume is unique because the word "vinegar" is substituted for "vineyard" in the Parable of the Vineyard. It is therefore known as "The Vinegar Bible." The third book is a museum piece called "The Treacle Bible" because it uses the word "treacle" (a kind of molasses) in place of the word "balm" in the quotation, "Is there no balm in Gilead?" THESE BOOKS ARE OF GREAT VALUE.

"Well!" said Bill. "Evidently the treasure hidden in this house is beyond even the imagination of gossips!"

"I'll look at the plans again and double-check my hiding place," prompted his cousin.

The Traceys hurried downstairs to look at the architect's drawings which had been left on the hall floor. Kay gazed around in bewilderment.

"The plans are gone!" she exclaimed.

IV

Stolen Plans

"Betty! Wendy!" shouted Kay.

Her voice rose shrilly to the high ceilings, then echoed through the empty rooms. At the cry of alarm the twins came running downstairs. Betty still clutched the precious antique Bibles. Wendy was trembling with fear.

"W-what's the matter?" they stammered.

"Somebody has stolen the plans," explained Bill briefly.

"Stolen them? Why, who could have done that?" gasped Betty. "No one was here except ourselves!"

"There's something strange going on here," replied Bill grimly.

Kay, who had run to the front porch, came back to say that no footprints or wheel tracks were to be seen on the driveway.

"Then someone's hiding in the house!" declared Bill Tracey. "We may find him if we hurry."

"Maybe you won't find *him*, but *her*," corrected Betty. "Remember that woman we saw here."

"I don't see her green car," called Wendy, surveying the driveway and the road from a side porch.

"We must search the house immediately," insisted Bill.

"It's such a rambling old place that it will take a long time to go through it," said Kay.

"You girls stay together for safety's sake," warned the lawyer. "Look around the first floor while I take the basement," he directed, hurrying toward the kitchen.

His quick footsteps thumped loudly across the bare boards of the hall, then were heard only faintly from the distant servants' quarters. Meanwhile Wendy stood still, frightened into thinking aloud. Betty heard her murmur:

> *"My heart's a drumbeat of alarm!*
> *I feel the chilly clutch of fear!*
> *Our feet are marching into harm*
> *Within this mansion's shadows drear!"*

"This is no time for poetry!" objected her twin, pulling impatiently at her sister's sleeve. "Come on, help us hunt!"

Reluctantly Wendy followed her companions. Keeping together, the three cautiously explored the den, the former music room, the long dining hall, the breakfast room and the ornate drawing room. Their search produced nothing but the scurrying of mice here and there. They went on into the kitchen.

Suddenly, the stillness was shattered by a loud Slam! Bang! Then came an ominous Thud! Thud! Thud! This was followed by the pounding of rapid footsteps. A hollow shout rose from the basement.

"Something has happened!" cried Wendy, turning white as paper.

"Bill has caught someone!" guessed Kay.

She rushed to a rear entrance. There was no sign of Bill, but through a window Kay caught a glimpse of a man running swiftly through brush and weeds into the dense woods back of the house. He seemed to be carrying a bundle under one arm.

"Bill, where are you?" called Kay.

A groan from below was the only answer. The twins paused uncertainly at the head of the basement stairway.

"He's hurt!" cried Betty.

"He's been killed!" moaned Wendy, blinking back tears.

"What happened?" called Kay, hurrying down the steep steps into the basement.

Bill got up slowly from the stone floor.

"I caught him but he got away!" the young lawyer said in disgust.

"Who got away?" demanded Kay.

"A man," Bill began. "Oh, my head!" He broke off abruptly, pressing both palms against his forehead.

"Can you get upstairs?" the twins asked anxiously.

"Yes, yes, I'm all right," he reassured them, trudging up the stairs unaided. "Someone was hidden right there in that corner behind the door at the top of these stairs," he explained. "As I started to go down, I turned and saw him. He wore a black mask over his face.

"He struck me but I grabbed him by the collar. We struggled a minute, then he tripped me. I lost my balance and he pushed me down the stairs and ran. It stunned me for a moment and he got away! It all happened so suddenly that I was taken by surprise!"

"Would you know him if you saw him again?" inquired Kay.

"No, I can't say that I would. His face was too well hidden. But I did notice that he had the plans."

"He did!" exclaimed Kay.

"Yes, they were on the floor and we stepped on them in the scuffle."

"He must have taken them with him, then, because they're gone now," announced Betty, looking carefully around for the lost diagrams.

"That's what the runaway man was carrying under his arm," Kay informed them. "I saw him dash into the thick woods behind the stables."

"There goes all the information about the hidden valuables," groaned Bill. "Now we can expect him to return to try to steal things."

"I think you ought to go home and put ice on that lump on your head," said Wendy sympathetically.

"I do, too," urged Betty, helping to brush the dust and cobwebs from Cousin Bill's clothes.

"And when we get back to town we ought to arrange to have the electricity turned on here. Then the house will light up and not leave so many dark corners as hideouts for prowlers," Kay suggested.

"More than that, I have to put a watchman on duty here immediately," Bill said. "And we must put those Bibles into the bank vault with the jewels. But first, Kay, take me to my office so that I can make arrangements for a watchman and notify Peter Greely of what has happened."

A telephone call to the airfield brought the disappointing news that Peter Greely had left on a secret mission for the government. No information as to his whereabouts could be given out.

"That's because it's a confidential matter involving an international airplane deal with England," Bill explained to the girls. "But it means additional responsibility for me during his absence!"

"Meanwhile I'm going to get a man to turn on the lights in the Greely Mansion at once," Kay announced.

"You attend to that while I report the theft of the

plans to the police," Bill answered.

Shortly after noon an employee of the electric light company was trailing the girls in his service truck to the deserted mansion.

"You certainly do need a little light out here," the man said, looking over the residence. "Too many cubby-holes to be safe in the dark."

The electrician was soon tinkering with the long unused meter and replacing broken bulbs in room after room.

"There you are, bright as day!" he announced at last.

The girls heard him depart, banging the door behind him. His truck went rumbling down the hemlock lane.

"Now that he's gone, let's leave, too," Wendy begged nervously. "I hate to be left here without some strong man. Suppose that prowler returns!"

"There are three of us," said Betty stoutly.

"We'll go in a minute," conceded Kay. "I just found this roll of old wallpaper. Before I forget, I'm going to try to draw a plan of this house on it and put in as many of those 'X' marks as I can remember."

She spread the sheets of wallpaper out as she had done with the original plans. Turning the plain side of the paper up, she started to draw. The twins crouched on the floor beside Kay, interested in her attempt to restore the secret record.

"Here's that newel post I couldn't open," said Kay, sketching roughly and marking an "X" in place carefully.

"Put another 'X' here where your cousin was looking for the panel in the wall of the den," Betty reminded her friend, as she scanned the drawing critically.

"What's that funny noise?" Wendy asked fearfully.

"Somebody must be sneaking around in this house!" She had been listening uneasily and now confessed frankly, "I'm scared!"

"I don't hear anything," said Betty.

"I do!" admitted Kay. "But I think the sounds are being made by rats behind the partitions."

"I don't," Wendy contradicted.

"I hear it now," said Betty. "It's a kind of scraping sound."

"It's coming right this way," Wendy whispered tensely.

"Here it comes! Let's hide!" said Betty.

Scampering quickly, the girls hustled into a hall closet. Outside there was the stealthy pad, pad, pad of muffled footsteps, accompanied by a click, click on the hardwood floor. Kay opened the door a crack.

"Why, it's a big animal!" she whispered.

"A wolf!" Wendy gasped, smothering a shriek.

"No, no!" said Kay in relief. "It's a German Shepherd!"

The twins peered out and saw the animal coming down the hall. It gazed about furtively, tipped its head up and gave a few inquiring sniffs. Then it dropped its nose to the floor and bounded directly toward the closet. Tilting its head sideways, the dog cocked its ears, and whined.

"Don't open the door. That thief may be with him," begged Wendy.

At the sound of her whisper the dog barked so loudly that both twins jumped. Kay quietly drew the door shut before the animal's nose. This excited the beast which broke into a deep-throated barking. Inside the dark closet the twins clutched each other nervously.

"Good dog, lie down," coaxed Kay in low tones through the keyhole.

The animal refused to be quiet. It bayed noisily

and flung its heavy body violently against the door. Its coarse nails scratched the thin panelling. Finally the big dog lay down with a thump, and snarled.

"We'll have to wait until he goes away," decided Kay.

"But he may keep us here all night!" wailed Wendy.

"He seems to be settling down to do just that," agreed Betty, "and it is stifling in this closet. There's no air!"

"Maybe this dog isn't really dangerous," said Kay. "I'm going out," she proposed, opening the door a crack.

A savage, guttural snarl from the unfriendly canine was its threatening answer.

"Come back!" Wendy shrieked.

V

On Guard!

While the girls remained prisoners inside the closet, Bill was being interviewed by Captain Wright, chief of the Brantwood police.

"You say the man who struck you wore a mask?" asked the officer, making note of Bill Tracey's answers. "Can you describe him?"

"Not very well. The black mask hid his entire face. Even his mouth was covered," the lawyer answered. "He was tall and athletically built, judging from the way he sprang at me."

"Thin or heavy?" asked the captain, carefully writing down the description in his notebook.

"Slender, strong and active," Bill replied thoughtfully, "and I think he was young. That's all I can tell you about him."

"This will give us a clue," the chief assured him. "I'll put detectives on the case immediately."

"And I'm hiring a watchman to guard the property," Bill added.

"Good idea. Are you getting Tom Curran?"

"Yes, he was very dependable in that mystery Kay solved concerning the Sacred Feather," he answered.

"Your young cousin was very clever in handling that case," Captain Wright approved heartily, "and Tom's a good man for that kind of a job."

"I'm driving Curran out to the Greely mansion right away," said the attorney, rising. "Let me know just as soon as you learn something about our burglar."

With the assurance that this would be done as soon as possible, Bill Tracey went to meet the watchman. They drove quickly toward the mansion.

Curran was a big, powerful man who inspired confidence by his strength and alertness. "I remember old man Greely very well," he said, as the two rode along. "I used to go out there to act as guard while he was still living."

"So you've been there before and are familiar with the grounds," remarked Bill Tracey. "All the better! You'll find your way around the place easily."

"I know every inch of the estate and the house from top to bottom," Tom replied. "I was often called in as watchman because the old man had an idea everybody wanted to rob him."

"Maybe they did." The lawyer chuckled. "I hear that many people envied him his wealth."

"Well, he was pretty sharp in his business deals," Tom explained. "While they say he was always strictly honest, he managed to get the best of every scheme. There were a good many people who resented it and tried to get revenge."

"Somebody's attempting to get something from his old home now," Bill asserted grimly.

He drove faster as his anxiety grew about the girls, whom he had not intended to leave alone so long. Suddenly an enormous truck which had been rumbling ahead of them on the narrow dirt road came to an abrupt stop as a tire went flat.

"Now how are we going to get past that?" asked Bill in disgust.

The truck blocked the road so that no automobile could get around it. On one side was a deep ditch and on the other the ground slanted sharply, down a steep hill. Bill Tracey and his companion got out of their car and strolled over to watch the truckdriver struggle with the giant tire. It was obvious that the job could not be finished in a hurry. Bill Tracey paced back and forth impatiently.

"I don't like this delay," he said to Tom. "I'm worried about my cousin and her friends being alone in that mansion. The man in the mask may come back."

Tom Curran nodded. "Probably he will," he agreed. "It certainly isn't very safe there!"

While this delay was taking place, the three girls were huddled uncomfortably in the stuffy closet. The dog lay by the door, growling at the slightest sound.

After what seemed an endless length of time the truck was repaired and started forward again. A short distance along the road Bill Tracey was able to pass it. He stepped on the gas and tried to make up for lost time.

"Everything looks serene," he said, drawing up in front of the Greely entrance and bounding up the steps.

As if to offset his remark, a ferocious barking greeted them, and faint cries of "Help!" sounded in muffled tones from the closet. The twins were calling to him, while Kay even ventured to push the door open an inch. With a growl the dog leaped against the wood. It slammed shut, and the girls were imprisoned again. The animal now turned on the newcomers, its teeth bared and the hair along its neck standing up.

Tom Curran walked briskly forward with no sign of fear. He drew his revolver. At his determined approach the dog slunk back, retreated, then bounded out the open rear door.

"Kay! Betty! Wendy!" Bill shouted anxiously.

"Here we are!" answered his cousin, tumbling from her prison, flushed and dishevelled.

The two men rushed forward. Inside the closet Betty unwound her legs from their cramped position and limped out, wincing at the "pins and needles" prickling her feet. Wendy tried to rise but slumped down, her back against the wall. Her head drooped limply to one shoulder.

"She's faint," warned Kay.

Bill lifted the girl out and laid her down gently in the hall. He forced open a window and said, "Take a deep breath!" Wendy did so, but closed her eyes.

"Here's some good cold water from the spring in the garden!" boomed Tom Curran's hearty voice.

He strode forward with a dripping bucketful. A long drink and a cooling splash on face and wrists soon restored Wendy. She sat up, pushing back her damp hair.

"I'm so glad you came!" she said gratefully. "What happened to the dog?"

"He ran away," replied Betty.

"Do you think he belongs to the man in the black mask?" Kay asked Bill Tracey.

"I wouldn't be surprised if he does," her cousin answered.

"I hope they come back because I'm waiting for them!" declared Tom Curran.

"The man is sure to return now that he has the directions for finding the valuables," Bill remarked regretfully.

"Oh, Bill, I was drawing a diagram of the house and its hiding places when the dog came!"

"Here is your sketch, Kay," said Betty, rescuing it from behind the closet door.

"I'm afraid it got torn," said Wendy.

"Never mind, it's still clear enough," answered Kay, smoothing out her wallpaper sketch to show to the men.

"I'm not surprised to hear that old Mr. Greely hid his valuables in all sorts of nooks and crannies," said Tom Curran. "He was obsessed with the idea that everyone wanted to rob him. He was exactly the kind of person who would go creeping about hiding his possessions like Easter eggs! He wouldn't even trust them to a safe deposit box in a bank."

"He seems to have had a collection of all kinds of valuables," observed Bill.

"Yes," said Kay. "First we find diamonds, then early editions. I wonder what else he had and whether he hid any money?"

"Maybe not much cash," suggested Tom. "He didn't believe in putting all his wealth into one form of security. He thought it was safer to have some investments in diamonds, and other possessions and some in the form of stocks and bonds or other things. Then, if the value of one should drop, that of another might rise and he wouldn't lose out altogether. He was a smart old man."

"What else do you suppose he collected and hid away?" speculated Kay.

"Nobody knows," replied Tom. "Almost any object that had real value, I suppose. And to think that all the time I was watchman here I never dreamed the walls were lined with treasure!"

"I had heard of it but didn't believe it," confessed Bill. "It took Kay's finding the jewels and the plans to convince me!"

"I heard there was no will," said Curran. "Is that right?"

"There is no will, so far as we know," Bill informed him. "Therefore, the estate goes to Peter Greely as nearest of kin."

"Maybe his great-uncle made a will and hid it!" suggested Kay shrewdly.

"That's an idea," said Tom Curran, "though I doubt if he left anything to his grandnephew. He didn't have any use for that young man. Furthermore Peter never paid any attention to him."

"Suppose Peter inherits everything, and then a will turns up later leaving the fortune to someone else," Kay conjectured.

"Don't suggest such a legal tangle!" moaned Bill.

"If a will ever is found," Tom stated positively, "I don't believe young Greely will be left a cent. It would be just like the old gentleman to give his money to some crazy scheme such as a home for aged canary birds!"

"Canary birds!" the twins shrieked.

"Yes, he was crazy about them." Tom Curran laughed. "He had dozens of them. Cages used to hang all around here," he explained, waving his hand toward the walls. "Oh, and he had grand furniture and beautiful paintings! This place was just like an art gallery. There were souvenirs and curios from foreign countries displayed in cabinets everywhere. And all the time those birds made a great racket singing, and cheeping, and whistling, and they kept scattering seeds all over the oriental rugs. Yes, Manuel Greely was a strange one!"

"He certainly sounds like it!" agreed Kay.

"So you found the plans in the stairs, eh?" Curran remarked curiously. "Why don't we pry up the rest of the steps all the way to the attic and make a thorough search for anything that may be hidden there?"

"We may as well," Bill agreed.

The men set to work wrenching open more steps until they both grew weary. They didn't find anything!

"It's getting late," said Bill at last. "We'll have to stop for tonight."

"But we can have light now," said Kay, snapping a switch. "It was hooked up a while ago."

Nevertheless Bill thought they should go home. "We'll leave you here on guard, Curran," he said.

"Take care of yourself," Wendy added.

"Don't worry about me!" Tom assured her, walking to the front of the house to say good night to the group.

Suddenly, the tread of feet sounded on the porch outside. In another instant there was the shrill ring of the long idle doorbell!

"Who can that be!" wondered Kay.

Tom Curran stepped forward and opened the door. A tall, muscular looking man stood there. He wore riding clothes and his rugged face was tan. He removed his broad-brimmed felt hat and introduced himself.

"I'm Clarence Cody," he said. "I believe I'm the new owner of this place!"

VI

A Costly Accident

"How do you do?" said Bill, stepping forward to introduce himself. "I'm Tracey, the attorney you've had correspondence with in regard to the purchase of this property. I wired you that new developments had arisen which might prevent the sale of this property. Apparently my telegram didn't reach you."

"You mean you don't intend to sell after all?" roared Clarence Cody indignantly.

"That may be the case," assented Bill.

"You mean to say I've come all the way East on a wild goose chase?" demanded Cody angrily.

"I'm afraid so," Bill Tracey nodded.

"The whole thing sounds crooked to me!" raged the disappointed ranchman. "What do you mean, something has come up to prevent the sale at the last minute? What is it?"

"Complications in the matter of ownership," answered the lawyer as straightforwardly as possible. "As you know, the owner died without leaving a will, and something has just come up that makes it a problem as to whether I have a right to sell in the absence of the heir."

"And where is this heir? Why can't we get in touch with him and settle the matter?" demanded the caller in fury.

"He's abroad at present and I can't reach him for some time."

Clarence Cody stormed up and down the hall, his fists crammed deep in his pockets, his boots clumping on the bare floor. His face glowered. Bill Tracey expressed regret for what had arisen. No one else in the group said anything. Each realized that if Cody knew the house contained a hidden fortune he might be more insistent than ever in forcing his end of the bargain.

Kay relieved the tense situation by introducing herself and saying sympathetically, "I know it's very unfortunate for you, Mr. Cody, and we're sorry that you made your long trip for nothing. You must be tired. Why don't you come home with us and have dinner? That will give you a chance to rest before you talk over this problem," she suggested.

"Afterwards we can hold a conference in my office and try to clear up the matter," added Bill, glad of a chance to delay a final decision.

Clarence Cody's scowl vanished. "Perhaps that would be the best thing to do," he agreed. "I'll take advantage of your kind invitation," he thanked Kay.

"Then we'll leave you in charge here, Curran, and go back to town," said Bill.

"I'll take care of things, don't worry," responded Tom, winking one eye confidentially.

"Do you have a car, Mr. Cody?" asked Kay, as they went outdoors.

"No, I flew in. I walked out here from Brantwood."

"You walked all that distance?" asked Betty.

Clarence Cody smiled for the first time since his arrival. "You must remember I come from the wide open spaces," he chuckled. "Why, my ranch is so far off the beaten track that we never see a bus or hear a train whistle!"

"That sounds exciting!" said Betty.

"It sounds lonesome to me!" shivered Wendy.

Not until Mr. Cody was seated at the dinner table in the Tracey home did he cheer up once more.

"Hot biscuits!" he cried in delight. "I haven't tasted any since I left home, and are they good!" He helped himself so liberally that he apologized for being greedy.

"Never regret having flattered the cook!" Mrs. Tracey laughed, hurrying to the kitchen to take a second tinful of biscuits from the oven.

Meanwhile Bill heaped chicken onto the guest's plate. Later, when Kay was drying dishes, she said to her mother:

"He certainly enjoyed his dinner and it put him in a good mood!"

Mrs. Tracey laughed. "Never talk business with a man before he has eaten," she advised wisely. "Always feed him first!"

"I guess you're right, Mother," Kay conceded. "I can hear him talking business with Bill very calmly and pleasantly now."

Bill Tracey's diplomatic replies continued to be evasive; he would not give any definite statement or promise. Finally Clarence Cody left, satisfied that the deal was not in any way questionable, and that it might be eventually settled to his advantage.

The following Monday morning Kay told the outcome to her friends. They were delighted.

"I sure hope the police catch that man who took the plans of the Greely mansion so you can find the treasure and sell the house to poor Mr. Cody," said Wendy kindheartedly.

"Even without the plans we could hunt," added Betty.

"Not today, though," Kay reminded them. "This afternoon we go to the perfume factory. Remember?"

"A trip through the Boswell Plant to observe the workings of commercial chemistry," Betty recalled in the words of the teacher, Doctor Staunton.

At the appointed hour the students climbed aboard the chartered buses. Kay and the twins joined the noisy crowd. There was a lot of laughter and talk, and one voice rang out louder and more insistent than any of the others.

"You can always hear Chris Eaton trying to make people believe she's important," grumbled Betty.

Chris continued to demand attention in her high-pitched voice. She crowded into the seat with one of the most popular boys, Ronald Earle. His friendly hello to Kay as she passed down the aisle indicated that he would have preferred sitting with her rather than share a seat with the Eaton girl. Chris ignored Kay, and informed all who would listen that she had met a very attractive cowboy.

"Just think!" she babbled on, "he's actually going to turn that old Greely dump into a Western ranch! Only it will be much more modern than those they have in the West!"

Some of the boys burst out laughing at this last foolish remark, and Chris gave them a dirty look.

"How in the world could she have met Mr. Cody already?" puzzled Kay.

"Her aunt has a ROOMS FOR TOURISTS sign in a front window," Betty informed her in a low voice. "Maybe he stayed there and Chris met him through her aunt."

"Probably," acknowledged Kay. "Anyhow, she knows his plans. Just listen to her!" she laughed.

Chris was prattling on nonstop. "You never saw anyone so handsome in your life!" she raved.

"Is he going to teach you to ride, Chris?" asked a girl at the other end of the bus.

"Positively!" Chris shouted back. "I'm crazy about horses and he's going to have the most exciting riding club!" she chattered on.

"You girls up there must join with me. Think of the adorable riding clothes we'll wear!"

Chris carefully excluded Kay and the Worths from all her plans. She was so enthusiastic during the entire trip, however, that five other girls actually promised to make up a riding group at the first possible chance.

"Imagine! Arranging all that when the Greely estate isn't even for sale anymore," muttered Betty indignantly.

"Sh!" warned Kay. "Don't let Chris suspect why the place isn't for sale. Just imagine the trouble she would make!"

"Yes," Wendy whispered. "Can't you see her snooping around in the mansion, trying to find treasure that doesn't belong to her?"

"We'll keep everything a secret from her," agreed Betty, "but I hate to have to listen to her!"

"You won't have to listen anymore," said Kay. "We're at Dunbar City, right in front of the factory."

"I can smell the perfume already," declared Betty, sniffing the air.

"How poetic to live in a town that is always sweet with the fragrance of roses and violets," said Wendy, dreamily. She immediately began to compose a poem about the loveliness of the air.

The students swarmed out of the buses and lined up for their trip through the Boswell Perfume Factory. Doctor Staunton introduced Mr. Lubin, manager of the plant, who led the way into the laboratories. As he conducted the visitors through the building, he paused to explain the chemical processes of the industry.

Chris Eaton, still fascinated with the subject of the riding club, could not bring her attention to the man's words. She kept up a stream of conversation in a buzzing undertone until finally the teacher was obliged to speak sharply to her for quiet. At his reprimand Chris sulked, refusing to concentrate on the exhibits being explained. Mr. Lubin overlooked the disturbance and addressed himself to the more attentive students.

"The making of perfume," he began, "is one of the oldest of the fine arts. As far back as we can trace religious ceremonies, perfume, usually in the form of incense, was used. The industry is now expanding in this country, though in the past America has not excelled in this particular art."

"Where did it come from, then?" someone asked.

"From Cyprus, China, Peru, Burma and Zanzibar," answered the manager, "and, of course," he added, smiling, "from my own country, France."

"Cyprus, China, Peru, Burma and Zanzibar," Wendy repeated dreamily. "That sounds like a poem in itself."

"There are three kinds of perfumes," Mr. Lubin continued. "Vegetable, artificial and animal."

"Will you please explain them?" asked Ronald.

"Yes, certainly. In vegetable perfumery we distil the delicate scent from the flowers themselves—from real violets, roses, lilacs, heliotrope and others."

"Lovely," murmured Wendy, whose thoughts were more on the poetry of sweet odors than on their chemistry.

"In this process a ton of rose petals yields only a few ounces of fragrant oil," Mr. Lubin went on.

"Must be an expensive process," observed one of the boys.

"Exactly. For that reason we now manufacture artificial scent from coal tar preparations. In this way we can make a product for four dollars which formerly cost us two hundred and forty.

"Next there are perfumes using an animal base. One of these is produced in this factory."

"What is that?" Kay asked with interest.

"Ambergris. This is a soft, waxlike substance found floating on the ocean. It comes from sperm whales who get sick from eating too many cuttlefish."

"That must be a whale of an odor!" one of the boys remarked, which caused an outburst of laughter among the students.

"Ambergris," continued the manufacturer, smiling, "is amber-gray in color and has a rather nice, earthy odor."

"How do you use *that* in the manufacture of perfume?" asked Kay, puzzled.

"When a sweet scent is exposed to this wax, it preserves the fragrance a long time. After the oil from the flowers has penetrated it fully, the ambergris is dissolved in alcohol as you see in this glass container."

The students crowded closer to see and sniff.

"Ambergris is so rare just now that the amount here is worth hundreds of dollars," stated the chemist.

Kay, who was nearest the speaker, gazed in awe at the big container, but Chris shrugged impatiently. Whether she jostled Kay is not certain, but, as Kay turned in the narrow aisle, she accidentally bumped the valuable jar. It toppled from the shelf and crashed to the floor!

VII

A Bag of Coins

At the sound of the crash, Mr. Lubin turned and saw the catastrophe. He was dismayed! Doctor Staunton offered contrite apologies for a member of his class causing such damage. Poor Kay was extremely upset.

"What can I do to replace this?" she asked sadly.

"It is impossible to replace just now!" declared the annoyed manager sternly. "Ambergris is hard to obtain these days."

Kay's spirits were crushed. It did not help her feelings any to see the sly smile on Chris Eaton's face. That girl always envied Kay. Now she could not suppress a feeling of jubilation at Kay's misfortune.

"Mr. Lubin, I'm very, very sorry," Kay said. "I promise you that somehow, some day, I will make up for what just happened!"

Her straightforward statement, without any attempt to say that it was not her fault or to place the blame on someone else, impressed the manager.

"Accidents will happen," he conceded.

Doctor Staunton gathered his class together and arranged to leave. The whole outing was dampened by the mishap.

Kay entered the bus with the others, but she was silent on the trip back to Carmont. When the

Brantwood students left for home, she was still determined to make good the loss she had caused. "But how?" she kept asking herself hopelessly. It seemed impossible, but Kay vowed that she *would* accomplish it! Her thoughts were rudely interrupted by the sudden, noisy chatter of Chris Eaton.

"Why, Mr. Cody!" she shrieked. "Fancy meeting you here! How perfectly delightful!"

"Clarence Cody has come aboard and you should see Chris falling all over herself to play up to him!" Betty muttered in disgust.

Kay did not bother to look in Chris's direction; yet she could not help overhearing her effusive greeting.

"Tell me, are your plans for the wonderful ranch complete? I can hardly wait to begin riding! I adore horses!" she gushed.

The man's deep voice rumbled some reply and Chris chirped, "Oh, do you really think you'll be able to make a horsewoman out of me? I love to ride, but I'm too timid to go out alone," she declared in an affected manner.

The rancher evidently suggested that she might enjoy the novelty of wearing Western riding clothes, because Chris now burst out with a ripple of laughter, crying:

"Oh, how too, too wonderful! Cowgirl outfits! What a unique touch that will give your ranch! Oh, I'm dying to have my picture taken in a cowgirl outfit, aren't you?" she asked her schoolmates.

Betty's face expressed supreme disdain and she nudged Kay with one elbow. The latter, again lost in thought about the spilled ambergris, hardly noticed her friend's gesture.

Kay's preoccupation lasted all through the next day, especially in chemistry class. Her mind wandered so much that she did poorly in her work. After school, however, Bill roused her from her gloom. He insisted that she accompany him to the mansion to see if Tom Curran had anything to report.

"No! No burglars or spooks!" the watchman laughed. He met the Traceys on the front porch which he was sweeping.

"I see you've been cleaning up around here," remarked Bill approvingly.

"Yes, I swept the house and the porches, raked up some dead leaves and trash, pulled a few weeds, and trimmed some of the bushes near the windows. I'll cut the lawn and get the place in good shape if I'm here long enough," he promised.

"You'll be here until we can clear up the mystery of the hidden fortune and give Peter Greely his legal rights," Bill replied.

"Tom," asked Kay, "haven't you heard anything unusual at all in the house, and hasn't that woman or the masked man tried to return?"

"Not so far as I know," responded the watchman. "While I was dusting upstairs I did think a couple of times that I heard someone meddling around down here. But each time, when I went to look, nobody was there and nothing seems to have been disturbed."

"You'll have to keep a lookout for a while," said the lawyer. "Perhaps you had better take my car now and go to town to buy supplies so you'll be stocked up."

Tom was glad to have the opportunity, and soon was driving to Brantwood while the Traceys inspected the mansion together.

"I'm convinced that it's only a matter of time before the man with the mask comes back to check out the hiding places marked on those plans he stole," asserted Bill.

He strolled off to the rooms. Kay, left alone, had a sudden inspiration.

"I am sure there was an 'X' marked on the floor under the place where Tom says old Mr. Greely's bed used to stand," she said to herself.

She ran along the upper hall to the huge chamber which had once been the owner's bedroom.

"Now, let me see," meditated Kay, eyeing the place critically. "The bed stood here."

She paced the floor, scrutinizing every board. In keeping with the old-fashioned ornamental woodwork, the floor was laid in an intricate pattern of squares of highly polished woods. Kay dropped to her knees and examined every inch of space. She ran her fingertips along the edges of each square in the pattern and along all the cracks. She had just concluded that she was wrong when a polished block suddenly moved under her touch!

"I'm just imagining it!" Kay told herself, but her quick fingers easily pried loose the square.

It lifted up, as if it were the lid of a box, and revealed an opening below! Hardly daring to believe her good luck, she plunged a hand into the dark hole. Her fingers touched something that felt like cool, smooth leather. She picked it up and found it was a man's wallet!

Kay was so absorbed in this discovery that she did not hear footsteps approaching until they reached the bedroom door. At the sound she jumped up hastily, hiding the purse under her sweater. Fearfully she looked at the door, fully expecting to face the black mask of the mysterious prowler.

"Oh, Bill, it's only you!" she gasped. "What a relief!"

"What are you hiding so guiltily?" he laughed.

"Look!" urged Kay, handing him the flat pocket-book. "I found it in a hole in the floor, and you startled me before I had time to look in it!"

Bill opened the wallet. Before their astonished eyes *one hundred-dollar bill after another fell out!*

"Five hundred dollars!" announced her cousin, amazed.

"I wonder if there is any more money in that spot?" Kay said excitedly.

Hastily she felt in the hiding place again. This time her hand struck a lumpy mound of stiff canvas, which she lifted out carefully.

"It's heavy!" she cried.

"A money bag!" Bill exclaimed.

"What's in it?" demanded Kay eagerly. "Gold!"

"No, I don't think so; just silver, dimes and quarters," reported her cousin, putting his hand into the bag and feeling the coins. Kay looked so disappointed that her cousin laughed out loud. "You are getting miserly when only gold will satisfy you!" he chided.

"Quick, hide it! Someone's coming!" Kay cautioned as a thunderous knock was heard on the front door.

Another, even louder, followed. Bill Tracey hastily handed the wallet and money sack over to Kay and ran downstairs to answer the heavy pounding. A sour-faced, middle-aged man stood there.

"I'd like to speak to Mr. Manuel Greely!" he demanded crisply.

Bill Tracey stared at the speaker, too surprised to answer.

"Don't stand there gaping at me!" snapped the caller. "I told you I want to see old man Greely!"

"Mr. Greely has been dead and buried for some time," Bill Tracey informed him.

The stranger's face was a study in baffled rage. "Well, that saves him a hot argument with me!" he snarled. "I came here to demand money he owes me!"

"Can I be of assistance?" Bill asked. "I'm the lawyer for the estate."

"Well," said the man dubiously, "I am due some money on a deal Mr. Greely put over on me once. I used to own a small candy shop in Denver, and I wanted to sell. A poorly dressed man approached me one day in regard to the sale and offered me a small sum to buy me out. He said he could afford no more and I believed him. I let him have the business for what he offered.

"Then what do you think? I found out that the guy was not a poor man at all but a slick agent of Greely's. No sooner did Greely get my concern than he built it into a big business. The place made him a fortune. Finally he sold out and made a mint of money in doing so. I asked him to let me share in the profits he had tricked me out of. But the old skinflint refused. At last I found I could come East to fight the matter out with the old pirate, only to find him dead and gone! He slipped by me after all!"

Meanwhile, hearing this, Kay had joined her cousin at the door.

"My legal response to you is that you have no claim on the Greely estate whatsoever," said Bill Tracey firmly. "You may have been annoyed, but there is not a cent due you under the law."

"Then the law's crooked like everything else!" roared the candy man in fury.

He stamped indignantly off the porch and departed, grumbling to himself. On his way down the steps he passed two girls who came scampering up. They pranced into the mansion without so much as a ring or a knock at the door.

"Chris Eaton and Marjorie Brown!" exclaimed Kay in surprise.

"Yes," answered Chris coolly. "We're joining the

Cody Cowboy Club and have come to look the place over," she announced airily.

The girls stalked indoors as if they owned the place.

"Mr. Cody isn't here right now," said Kay.

"He'll be along pretty soon," said Chris. "We have a date with him! After all, this is his property, so why, may I ask, are you trespassing?"

"My cousin, Bill Tracey, is in charge of the sale and we are here on a business matter," Kay answered stiffly.

"Oh, indeed? Very important, aren't you?" sniffed the disagreeable girl. "Come on, Marge," she continued, "let's go outside. I want to show you the marvellous stables. Isn't this place going to be fabulous when Mr. Cody gets it fixed with a lot of Wyoming atmosphere?"

Without another word to Kay, Chris conducted her friend on an inspection of the grounds.

"Quick, let's get the money!" Kay whispered to her cousin. "I brought it down and hid it in the den."

The lawyer had just seized the canvas bag when a shout at the door announced the arrival of Cody himself! Startled, Bill Tracey let the bag slip from his fingers. Out poured the coins noisily! Dimes and quarters rolled wildly over the floor.

Leaving Bill to collect them, Kay dashed from the room. She closed the door so Mr. Cody could not see this unexpected display of silver.

"How do you do?" she greeted the ranchman a little breathlessly. "Chris and her friend are out at the stables waiting for you!" she announced.

Clarence Cody good-naturedly swung off in the direction of his future customers. Kay raced back to help gather up the spilled money.

Both the Traceys were groping about on the floor, fishing up runaway dimes and quarters from every nook and corner, when a terrible scream rang out from the stable yard.

"What's that?" gasped Kay.

Before Bill could guess at an answer, another shriek pierced the air, more agonizing than the first!

VIII

The Black Mask

As shriek after shriek rang out, Bill Tracey ran to find out what the trouble was. Kay stayed behind to finish picking up the last of the coins. She then returned the bag and wallet upstairs to their original hiding place.

"That's the safest spot I can think of for them," she reflected, as she carefully closed the opening of the square in the floor. "I wonder what happened outside."

The shrill cries of Chris and Marjorie were becoming wilder and wilder. The deep voices of Clarence Cody and Bill Tracey now joined in excitedly. Kay, running out to see what was the matter, was greeted by warning shouts.

"Back! Go back!" boomed Cody, madly waving his arms.

Chris and Marjorie, their faces covered by their arms, were rushing blindly toward the back entrance to the mansion.

"Yellow jackets!" bellowed Bill, fighting off the maddened insects which were buzzing around his head. "Chris ran into their nest and stirred them up!"

"And we're stung to death!" screamed Marjorie.

Chris was sobbing dramatically. Her face was red and swollen from the sting of a yellow jacket, but it was plain to Kay that Chris was playing up the situation.

"Oh, oh, I'm afraid I'll lose the sight of this eye!" she wept.

Clarence Cody tried to reassure her. "A little mud will relieve that!" he consoled her sympathetically.

"It hurts so, but I'm trying to be brave!" she declared with a phoney attempt to sound heroic.

"You *are* brave!" said Cody admiringly.

"She's just being dramatic to get his attention!" thought Kay in disgust, "and he's actually falling for it!"

"Oh, take me home!" Chris pleaded.

Cody solicitously helped Chris into her car, then took his place at the wheel. He had completely forgotten poor Marjorie who had to climb into the backseat unaided, despite the fact that she, too, had been stung. Snuggling close to the cowboy for comfort, Chris was secretly delighted as they drove away. Kay and Bill watched them go in deep relief.

"That takes Cody's mind off the delayed sale of this place," smiled the lawyer. "It's a good thing, since I haven't heard from Peter Greely and don't know what my next move should be."

While the two Traceys were discussing the situation, a masked figure crept stealthily out of the woods behind the stable! Nearer and nearer to the mansion it moved, as slowly as a cat stalking a bird. It crouched low in the thicket for a moment, then started to crawl through the tall weeds to the back of the house.

"Here comes Tom Curran!" Kay said at just that moment.

The watchman was returning from town in Bill Tracey's car. The motor made so much noise that no one heard the man in the black mask as he slipped indoors through a secret entrance.

"Hello, Tom, did you get everything you needed?" Bill called in such loud and hearty tones that nobody heard the creaking of the back stairs as the intruder slunk like a shadow up to the second floor.

There was now a great deal of talking and tramping back and forth while Tom Curran unpacked his purchases. Under cover of this bustle, the intruder reached the third floor. He leaned over the top banister to listen and chuckle softly. Then he swung himself up through an attic trapdoor into a snug hiding place beneath the roof. With a grin of satisfaction he settled down to bide his time for action. He hugged to him the stolen roll of the architect's drawings.

"I got coffee and canned goods and bread," Tom Curran was saying, "and this little broiler too, so I can keep house!" he laughed.

The two cousins looked over his selection. Then Bill said, "Come on, Kay, it's getting late. We should start for home."

Kay excused herself for a moment while she darted upstairs to get the money. She almost hesitated to open the secret square, afraid the treasure might have vanished during her absence! It was still safe, however, so she gathered it up and hurried back with it.

She did not dream that she had been one flight nearer the masked intruder! He, in turn, did not guess for a minute that there was one more spot marked "X," now empty.

With friendly good-byes to Tom the Traceys drove off. As their car lurched along the bumpy lane under the dark hemlock trees, a pair of eyes watched them go. High up under the attic eaves a man in a mask watched them through a small, cobwebbed window.

When the intruder was satisfied that the Traceys had gone, he climbed down like a monkey from the trapdoor and listened again over the banisters. All he could hear was Tom Curran moving about in the kitchen, whistling to himself. The eavesdropper now removed his shoes and adjusted his mask. In stocking feet he crept softly down the back stairs.

Tom could be seen at his new stove, making himself a cup of coffee and frying a piece of ham. The masked man squatted in a dim corner and watched his prey through the half-closed door. Finally Tom Curran stepped inside the pantry to get some bread and butter.

Like a flash the figure that had been lurking in the darkness leaped across the kitchen, and slammed the pantry door! A click of the key, and Tom was locked in! His captor snapped his fingers in satisfaction.

Curran let out a yell and started kicking so violently that he threatened to splinter the door. His jailer watched it anxiously for a minute, but the sturdy wood held fast. The prowler grinned wickedly. Wasting no more time, he took off his mask and carefully examined the red "X" marks on the plans he carried.

First he ran to the spiral stairway in the front hall. A glance at the torn-up steps angered him. Next he scaled the stairs with a few quick strides of his long legs. He went directly to the window seat where, in its secret compartment, the Worth twins had found the valuable editions of the ancient Bibles. Apparently someone had taken the booty before him! With a furious exclamation he consulted his guide again.

At that moment Kay Tracey returned to the house and called out to Tom. The intruder upstairs, startled by her voice, crouched hastily out of sight.

"T-o-m!" Kay shouted. "Why—what—!"

A thunderous uproar arose from the pantry.

"L-E-T M-E O-U-T!" yelled the prisoner, punctuating his shrieks with a fierce bombardment of kicks against the woodwork.

"Is that you in there, Tom?" called Kay.

"Yes, it's me!" bellowed the trapped watchman. "Unlock the door and let me out!"

"The key's gone!" Kay shouted back.

"Get a hatchet! Get the axe! Break it open!" howled Curran, thumping the panels impatiently with both fists. "Hurry up!"

"I'm trying to hurry," answered Kay, "but I don't see any of your tools. I'll run back and get Bill!"

"Tell him to hurry!" Curran pleaded.

Bill sprinted in response to Kay's frantic call for help.

"Where is Curran?"

"Locked in the pantry!" Kay answered, running in order to keep up with her cousin's swift pace.

Bill snatched a piece of old pipe that lay in a trash pile.

"Watch out for your head, Tom!" he cautioned. "I'm going to smash the door in!"

A few heavy blows and one of the panels gave way. Curran was able to squeeze out through the opening.

"Who locked you in there?" asked Kay in bewilderment.

"I dunno," answered Tom crossly. "After you folks left I stepped in here to get something, when bang! somebody slammed the door and turned the key!"

"Somebody must be hiding in the house!" cried Kay in alarm.

"How did you happen to come back here?" asked Tom, calming down somewhat, now that he was released. "If you hadn't, I might have been in there for some time."

"My car radiator leaked," Bill explained.

"I ran in to ask you where that spring is so Bill could get a pail of water," Kay added.

"Lucky for me!" observed Curran.

"We'd better search the place," urged Bill, beginning to look cautiously about him in the maze of passageways.

"Wait! Wait! Don't risk it alone," cautioned Tom. "Let's stick together. I have my gun so come on!" he added, leading the way.

The man hiding in the upstairs hall overheard this remark. Quickly he tied on his mask again, concealing his entire face. Tiptoeing in stocking feet he hurried along the upper hallway. As he heard footsteps coming upstairs he ducked into a back bedroom. On and on came the tramp of feet and the grumbles of Curran.

The thief sped nimbly from one room to another, as the approaching searchers got closer and closer! He tried to sneak ahead to reach his trapdoor hideaway but Kay unknowingly cut him off.

"Let's look here by the linen closet," she suggested.

The searching party turned immediately and thus blocked the intruder's escape to his attic refuge.

"Nobody here, but we'll get him yet!" declared Tom Curran determinedly.

The masked man ducked silently into another passageway. His heart was thumping painfully, as he realized that he was slowly being cornered. Like a rabbit pursued by hounds, he scrambled frantically to get away.

"Try down this way!" called Bill, exploring the rear wing of the mansion.

"You're getting warmer!" thought the intruder grimly. "Warmer and warmer, and you've almost got me—" he thought in a panic, "but—not quite!"

There was only one thing left for him to do. In a few minutes more the hunters would find their quarry. Who could tell what might happen? Fighting with his back to the wall like a wild animal, he decided to take a chance.

Still moving noiselessly, the desperate man climbed out of a back window. Some distance below him stretched the roof of a porch. It was a narrow one, offering little room for a wild leap from the high window above.

"But it's my only chance!" thought the man. At the sound of approaching footsteps he took his chance. He jumped recklessly onto the steeply slanting roof!

Kay heard a thud and rushed to look out of that very window! She was just in time to see the man slide perilously down the smooth shingles. He clawed the air frantically to stop his fall, and—*his mask slipped off!*

Kay shouted, "Here he is!"

At her cry the unmasked man turned and looked up. He and Kay gazed at each other for a fleeting moment!

IX

An Important Picture

The fleeing intruder slid to the edge of the rain gutter and swung himself to the ground. Before Tom Curran and Bill could chase him, the mysterious man vanished into the gloomy wood behind the barns.

"I saw him clearly," cried Kay. "I never saw him before, but I'm positive I'd know him if I ever saw him again!"

"I vow I'll get that man!" declared Tom Curran.

"Watch out that he doesn't sneak up on you again and do more than lock you in a closet!" warned Bill.

"Yes, be careful!" pleaded Kay.

"Don't worry," Tom reassured them. "Next time it will be Mr. False Face, not me, who gets locked up!"

As Kay and Bill were driving to Brantwood, she said soberly, "I can't help wondering if Curran will be safe all alone in that big empty mansion. It should be easy for that man to creep in on him in the night!"

Although Kay was very brave, she shivered at the thought of Tom Curran being overpowered by a robber.

"Tom's armed, and being a watchman is his business," replied Bill confidently. "He's an old hand at that game and usually gets his man. So don't worry about him."

Mrs. Tracey was waiting for them at the door when they returned.

"Late again!" she laughed. "I'm afraid the dinner is cold. I hope that whatever kept you was worth the time."

Kay smiled at her mother. "We've had such an exciting afternoon!" she explained. "It would be boring just to get to meals on time and never have any adventures!"

"I worry that so much adventure will give the whole Tracey family indigestion!" the girl's mother said with a smile. "But tell me about it."

Kay related all that had happened, including the discovery of the money and the attack on Tom Curran.

"Just think, Mother, when the man escaped down the roof I actually got a good look at him with his mask off! Now what, I ask you, is missing a hot meal compared with that kind of excitement! Though I admit you are the best cook in the world."

"It's too exciting to be safe!" objected her mother. "Where is this money you found?"

Bill produced the wallet and bag from his pockets.

"Count the coins," urged Kay. "I'm dying to know the amount. The bag is as heavy as lead!"

"No wonder!" answered her cousin, busily stacking dimes and quarters into separate little piles. "Guess how much?" he challenged, finishing the count.

"I give up!" laughed Kay. "Tell me and relieve the suspense!" she begged.

"Ninety-nine dollars!" announced Bill.

"Five hundred and ninety-nine all together," Kay exclaimed. "And just think, that is the loot from only *one* of those places marked with an 'X'. The plans were sprinkled with red marks."

"Good thing that the sale of the property to Cody

wasn't completed before we discovered all this!" said Bill.

"I can hardly wait to tell Wendy and Betty what they missed today!" Kay remarked.

"Be careful not to let any information get around at school about the old mansion being a gold mine," warned Bill.

"Don't worry," promised Kay. "I'll be discreet!"

Although she felt it was wise not to reveal the large amount of money discovered in the old house, she did tell her friends about the spectacle Chris Eaton had made of herself after her battle with the yellow jackets. The twins were disgusted when they heard how Chris had acted with Cody.

They were amazed by the story of the sneak thief's escape. The three girls were buzzing about this as they entered the school library during a study hour, but soon quieted down and soon were deep in reference books. Kay, quicker than the others, finished her assignment before the period was over. She filled in the rest of the hour by looking through a magazine. Suddenly her attention was caught by a picture in one of the advertisements.

It was a striking photograph of a magnificent police dog. The animal was looking imploringly at its master, who was opening a box. Beneath the picture was a line reading, "Give your pet Eatmor Dog Food. It keeps him in perfect health."

Kay could not take her eyes from the figures.

"Now what is it about this picture that fascinates me so much?" she wondered. Then in a flash she saw something familiar on the page. "That man feeding the dog!" she gasped.

In her surprise she spoke half aloud and the librarian lifted her head and frowned at the sound. Kay lapsed into silence but continued to stare at the print. When the bell rang, she went to the desk and signed up to borrow the magazine.

"Why are you taking only a magazine?" Betty asked, amused at Kay's choice.

Kay promptly backed the twins into a corner of the corridor and held the Eatmor advertisement before them.

"Look at that man!" she urged, her voice almost trembling with excitement.

"What about him?" inquired Betty, unmoved.

"He's extremely handsome!" responded Wendy admiringly.

"Do you know who he is?" demanded Kay.

"Never saw anybody like him before," the Worths replied.

Kay's voice rose with eagerness. "As sure as anything, *that's a picture of the intruder!*"

"Really?" whispered Betty in a flutter of surprise.

"Are you sure?" asked Wendy doubtfully.

"I'm positive!" retorted Kay. "I looked that man straight in the eye and this is a perfect photograph of him!"

At this moment Ronald Earle sauntered down the corridor.

"Hello there!" he greeted them. "What's all the talk about?" he inquired with a grin.

"Kay's admiring the handsome hero in a dog food ad!" laughed Betty.

Ronald's face clouded at these words. "What's this?" he demanded in mock seriousness. "Is he somebody you know?" He felt a twinge of jealousy when he saw how intently Kay looked at the man's picture.

"Yes, I think he is," began the girl uncertainly. "At least he looks exactly like someone I saw recently and certainly would like to see again!" Seeing the look of dismay on Ronald's face, she went on. "This is just another little detective job I'm trying to solve. I'll let you in on the secret."

Ronald seemed relieved at these words.

"I think this man in the picture is a person Bill is trying to locate in regard to a legal matter. We also think he owns a dog like that one. Now if I only knew who posed for this photograph or how to get in touch with the company which made the ad—"

"Oh, if that's all that's on your mind I can help you out!" Ronald announced confidently. "I know a man in Dunbar City who makes these photographs for advertising companies. I'm sure this is some of his work. I'll drive you to his office and we'll see if he can tell us who the good-looking model is."

"Ronald, that's wonderful!" exclaimed Kay so enthusiastically that Ronald beamed with pleasure.

Kay was delighted with her friend's clever suggestion and decided to tell Bill as soon as she saw him. Then on second thought she decided she would wait and surprise him if the scheme proved to be a success. It was just as well, for on arriving home, she found the lawyer in a predicament. Clarence Cody had just come in and was demanding that the sale of the Greely estate be completed at once.

"I made a trip all the way from Wyoming, don't forget, to close the deal," Cody stormed. "At first you seemed only too glad to sell the place as quickly as possible!"

Kay noticed Bill nod in agreement with the rancher's statement.

"Then all of a sudden, without any explanation, you begin to hem and haw and beat about the bush and delay this transfer," Cody accused. "Now, I ask you point blank, *why?* What's the reason for the delay?"

Bill Tracey drew a deep breath, started to speak, and thought better of it. He remained silent. This enraged Cody.

"I have a freight car of saddle horses due to arrive here in two days," Cody argued hotly. "I must have a place to put them. Now, are you going to let me have these stables as originally agreed? If not, what am I supposed to do with all my animals? The deal has to be settled, Mr. Tracey, and now!"

X

The Telltale Clipping

Kay saw that her cousin was in difficulty and wondered how she could help him. She was glad when he invited her into the room where he and Mr. Cody were standing.

"I have explained to you already," said the lawyer slowly to the ranchman, "that a matter has come up which makes it impossible to sell the Greely estate at present. Later, perhaps, this will be cleared up and the sale can go through."

"Then what am I going to do?" asked Clarence Cody.

Both men looked so perplexed that Kay offered a suggestion. "You wouldn't want to buy and afterward have to give it up, Mr. Cody. Cousin Bill, why not keep the mansion out of the bargain altogether and rent the stables?"

"But I want to use the house, too," objected the client.

"Mr. Cody," said Kay persuasively, "wouldn't it be a good idea to rent just the stables at first? Then you could give your ranch idea a try-out and see whether it is a money-making proposition. If it is, perhaps later on you could lease the house, or even buy the whole thing. If it's not successful, then you will have saved your money."

"There's something to what you say," agreed Cody reluctantly. "At any rate, it would solve the problem of what to do with the horses now."

"We could arrange that any rent paid could be applied on the purchase if that should go through later," added Bill, pleased at Kay's suggestion. "The property is extensive and you may use all of it. There must be ten miles or more of woods along the mountain road that would make interesting places for horseback trips."

This plan pleased Cody. "Yes, I'll agree to that," he said. "Fair enough. Looks as if I might be getting the best of the bargain at that! A very clever solution of a problem, young lady!" he said, smiling. "To show my appreciation for your helping me out in this matter, I'd like to give you some riding lessons free of charge!"

"I'd love it!" accepted Kay, beaming.

She told the good news to her friends on the way to school the next day.

"So Chris is not the only cowgirl we'll see galloping around!" laughed Betty.

"Kay, I can't wait to see you in a ten-gallon hat!" said Wendy with a ripple of laughter.

"Don't be silly! I'm not going in for anything like that!" promised Kay.

Wendy's imagination had been caught, and Betty noticed a familiar dreaminess in her sister's eyes. Sure enough, the poet began composing:

> *"Silver Pegasus is the horse with wings,*
> *A steed that has never ploughed,*
> *Mounted on him, Kay scorns the earth*
> *And soars to a shining cloud."*

"I can make up better poetry than that myself!" cried her twin. She closed her eyes in thought for a moment, then burst out:

"Astride a night mare Wendy rides,
I think of it with dread!
Her prancing steed may rear and kick
And toss her out of bed!"

"Oh, Betty!" exclaimed Wendy, both amused and provoked.

"Why don't both of you join me in riding?" urged Kay. "Chris is getting a group together, so let's make up our own crowd!"

"Do you see what I see?" Betty asked abruptly.

The friends had just reached Carmont High School. On the front steps was a sight that made Betty clap both hands over her mouth to keep from laughing aloud.

"It's Chris Eaton!" gasped Wendy in amazement.

"Dressed up like a cowgirl, from ten-gallon hat to chaps and spurs!" cried Kay.

Boys and girls were crowding around this picturesque figure, laughing, teasing, ridiculing, or admiring her. Chris's broad-brimmed felt hat was held on by a long leather thong drawn snugly under her chin. She wore a flaming red silk shirt and short leather vest studded with glittering metal disks. A yellow satin bandana was knotted jauntily around her neck. She strutted around in ornate, high-heeled riding boots.

"Chris does at least look striking," Kay remarked, "if nothing else."

One of the boys snatched the enormous hat and jerked loose her neckerchief in spite of Chris's shrieks. Amid laughter and cheers from other students, he dressed himself up and jumped on Ronald Earle's back, singing:

"Give me my boo-oo-oots and s-a-d—dle!"

Ronald began to leap about like a bucking bronco. Finally he flung his rider to the ground with a thump.

Chris's cowgirl costume gave so much publicity to Cody's plan that the next afternoon a crowd of students lined up along the railroad siding when the shipment of western horses arrived. The animals, cramped from their long trip, now reared and plunged, snorting and stamping as they were released from their close travelling quarters.

"They're a frisky bunch of horses!" Wendy commented. "We'd better look out."

A short, grisly stableman was struggling with a big, unruly animal. This groom, called Jimmy, was a comical looking figure who amused the onlookers.

"He's so bowlegged he looks like a croquet wicket!" snickered one of Ronald's friends.

"That's because he has ridden horseback ever since he could walk, I suppose," said Kay.

At this moment Chris roared up in her car, screeching to a stop. She leaped out nimbly and strode forward, shouldering aside her schoolmates. She was dressed in her spectacular cowgirl outfit. Pushing herself ahead, she spoke familiarly to Cody, who was too busy to give her any attention beyond a quick nod.

Chris now began showing how fond she was of horses. She made a great fuss about patting their noses, talking intimately with Jimmy about how the animals had stood the trip. Just at the moment when Chris was acting most superior, a horse rushed down the planking from the train, broke loose, and started kicking violently.

"Help! Help! Don't let him trample me!" Chris screamed.

As she ran wildly, her Stetson hat flew off, and one of her spurs caught on something that tripped her. She fell down in a humiliating heap!

"Chris is nothing but a show-off!" sniffed Betty. "Let's go."

Kay climbed in behind the wheel of the Tracey car and started the motor.

"Let's go before the procession gets started and tell Tom Curran they're bringing the horses to the stable," she suggested, driving in the direction of the Greely estate.

"I wonder if Tom has discovered anything more about the mansion?" speculated Betty as the girls pulled up at the big house.

"No, no more secrets as far as I've been able to find out," Curran replied, when the girls questioned him.

He seemed very glad to have visitors, and to know that Cody and the grooms were on their way to the stables.

"It's lonely out here, and it'll be a good thing to have more men on the place," said Tom.

"But Cody mustn't find out that the house has hidden treasure," cautioned Kay.

"Oh, of course not," Tom answered.

"Have you heard any more mysterious noises?" asked Wendy.

"Or caught a glimpse of the masked man?" added Betty.

"No mysterious noises and no masked stranger," Curran replied. "But I did find one thing. Look here!" He produced a newspaper clipping from his pocket. "I noticed this when I was cleaning up and came across a pile of papers," he explained.

Kay took the clipping, and Wendy and Betty leaned over her shoulder as she read:

"'Wealthy Man Brings Lawsuit.
Manuel Greely Sues Business
Competitor.'"

There was a faded picture of old Manuel himself in the courtroom opposite his opponent, who was described merely as J. J. Richman.

"I wonder," said Kay, "whether this Mr. Richman could possibly be our masked man?"

XI

The Moving Trapdoor

"What makes you think the man in this newspaper picture might be the masked intruder!" Wendy asked Kay.

"Because he may hold some grudge about the lawsuit and be trying to get back money he thinks belongs to him, like that candy man did."

"Can't you recognize him from the photograph?" asked Betty. "You got a good view of the man without his mask."

Kay frowned at the clipping and shook her head. "The features are too blurry."

She was still studying it when they heard the thunder of horses' hoofs.

"Here comes Cody's Cavalcade!" Wendy announced, rushing to a window.

A string of horses under the guidance of Cody and Jim, who were mounted, came pounding up the driveway.

"Quite a troop," Tom Curran said admiringly.

He and the girls hurried outside to watch as the animals were put into the roomy stables. One horse, more nervous than the others, suddenly broke loose and galloped off wildly across a field.

"That's the one that scared Chris!" cried Kay.

"It's Prairie Queen. I hope I can catch her!"

groaned Cody. "Somebody watch where she goes until I can ride after her!"

He rushed back and frantically helped Jimmy get the other animals into their stalls. In the midst of this confusion, Chris Eaton, still in her Western outfit, drove into the yard. One headlight of her car was broken. She said angrily that it had been smashed by a kick from Prairie Queen at the railroad siding.

In the meantime the runaway horse had stopped on the far side of a pasture. Calmly Queenie began to eat grass.

"She'll stay there and graze till we can catch her," Jimmy decided.

During all the commotion, nobody had noticed a stealthy, masked figure that crept unseen through a secret entrance and slunk softly upstairs. With steps as lithe and silent as a panther's, the man skulked up to the attic and swung himself confidently into his hiding place above the trapdoor.

This breathless moment had scarcely passed, when there came a clatter of footsteps downstairs. The sound of cheerful voices echoed upward toward that attic hole. Kay and the Worths had left the excitement out-of-doors and had come inside.

"This is a good chance to do a little searching," Kay told her companions.

Wendy suddenly said,

> *"I found some money, lost long ago,*
> *In the attic of an old house.*
> *Among rags and tags were green dollar bills,*
> *Woven into a nest—by a mouse!"*

"That's a little better than some of your efforts," conceded Betty in an offhand way. Then she asked, "Come on, Kay, where shall we look first?"

Wendy stood still. She was a little hurt by her twin's lack of interest in her poem. An idea had just flashed into her mind and she decided to investigate it alone, without saying a word either to her sister or to Kay.

While the other girls went to the den to search for the secret panel that Bill had failed to find, Wendy crept upstairs by herself. The idea of a nest of mice being in the attic reminded her that there had been a red "X Important" on the architect's plan of the third floor.

"It seems to me that the mark was right here somewhere," she thought, exploring the upper hall.

At the end of the corridor, near the top of the back stairs, was a closet. In the ceiling was the trapdoor behind which the masked stranger was crouching!

With no suspicion of the danger lurking so near her, Wendy pushed open the door and looked around inside the closet in search of some clue. She found nothing but an electric fuse box with switches controlling different sets of lights on the top floor of the mansion.

Wendy was busy fumbling about, when she heard a muffled cough! Startled, she froze and listened. Again there was the faint sound of a human being!

"Where could it have come from!" she wondered. She turned and looked sharply about her. The sound was repeated. It seemed to be very close by. "But nobody's here!" she thought uneasily. "I feel as if someone were standing right beside me, yet is invisible! It's weird!"

Trembling, Wendy ran her fingers fearfully along the woodwork.

"Someone must be hiding behind a secret panel here," she thought nervously. "I wish I'd waited for Kay and Betty!"

At that moment there was a sudden squeak

overhead! She glanced up and spied the trapdoor. To her horror it was opening!

Wendy jumped with fright and her hand struck an open switch on the fuse box. An electric shock as well as one of fear shot through her. She toppled unconscious to the floor!

The girl lay in a limp heap. She did not know that the sinister masked figure dropped cautiously out of the loft; that he gave her a suspicious glance, coughed softly, then swiftly tiptoed down the back steps just as Kay and Betty came bounding up the front staircase!

"Wen-dy! Where a-r-e you?" they called.

"I can't figure out where she went," Betty worried. "I wonder why she doesn't answer?"

By the time the girls reached the attic, they saw why she did not answer.

"Wendy!" cried Betty hysterically.

Her scream brought Tom Curran, who came running, revolver in hand. Kay, meanwhile, had dropped to her knees by the fallen figure.

"She's okay!" she reassured Betty. Kay slapped the unconscious girl's cold hands and patted her white cheeks sharply. "Wendy! Wake up! Answer me!" she kept demanding insistently.

Finally Wendy responded. She opened her eyes and gave a long, shuddering sigh.

"What happened?" asked Betty tearfully.

Wendy blinked her eyes in bewilderment. "Where am I?" she asked in a daze. It was several minutes before she could collect her wits. Instinctively her gaze went to the trapdoor in the low ceiling. "Oh, now I remember," she murmured.

"What? What do you remember?" pleaded Betty.

"It opened!" said Wendy, trembling with fear. "That door opened! I saw it! Someone was up there coughing! It was so scary!"

Tom Curran immediately swung himself aloft through the trapdoor.

"Be careful!" pleaded Wendy, her lips pale.

She hid her face on Betty's shoulder as Tom disappeared within the dark hole. His heavy footsteps could be heard tramping about over their heads. Soon his cheery voice called down:

"Nobody here now!"

"I think that hole ought to be nailed tight shut," said Kay as Curran jumped down.

"I do, too," agreed the watchman, going for hammer and nails to do it immediately.

Wendy now felt able to walk and asked to be taken home. The three girls went downstairs together, Kay and Betty supporting Wendy, who was still shaky. Halfway along the second floor hall Kay remarked about a place where the wallpaper was torn badly.

"It's a pity that this house is falling to pieces," she said. "This paper is so pretty and it's coming off in strips. I guess the plaster under it cracks with age and loosens it."

She ran one hand along the wall as she passed. Kay's fingers slid under the tear in the paper, and she felt a crack that was not plaster. It was of wood! With an exclamation she let go of Wendy and quickly stripped the torn covering from the wall. Ripping it away, she revealed a hidden door!

Kay and Betty tried their best to move this, but it would not budge. Poor Wendy looked as if she might faint.

"Don't open it!" she begged them. "Someone may be behind it!"

So nervous and unstrung had Wendy become, that the others decided it was best not to stop to investigate further.

"I'll get Tom to force it open later," said Kay.

"We sure are learning things about this weird old mansion!" said Betty excitedly.

Kay told Tom that they were leaving and hurried outdoors. She was going to bring her car to the door and take Wendy home at once.

As she ran along the weed-grown driveway, an alarming sight greeted her eyes. Racing across the distant pasture was the horse, Prairie Queen. In hot pursuit, snapping savagely at her heels, ran a wild gray animal!

"It's a wolf!" was Kay's first thought. Then, shading her eyes, and squinting to see better, the girl corrected herself. "No, she's being chased by that terrible dog that kept us shut up in the closet! *It's the Eatmor dog that belongs to the masked intruder!*"

The wolflike animal rushed on, leaping at the horse's flying heels. Now Prairie Queen was leaving the pasture and heading into the dark forest at the foot of the hills. Before Kay could call her owner, the animal had vanished into the dense woods, the dog still at her heels.

"She'll be lost!" gasped Kay, and ran in desperation toward the barn, shouting for Jimmy and Cody.

XII

Pursuit!

At Kay's excited cries, Cody flung himself onto a horse and galloped off. He waved his hand to signal that he understood the shouted directions.

"I must tell Tom about this," thought Kay excitedly, racing into the house. "If that dog belongs to the masked man, then he probably is around here himself!"

Tom looked grim when Kay told him her idea. She warned him not to alarm Jimmy, suggesting that he simply ask the stableman to let him know if he saw anyone around, because the person might be the unwanted dog's owner.

"I understand," nodded Tom. "Now you go on home and I'll look around here as if I had eyes in the back of my head as well as in the front."

Wendy was glad to get away from the mysterious mansion for a while, but said she would like to come again to find out what was behind the newly discovered door.

"All right. I can't come back myself tomorrow because I'm going with Ronald to Dunbar City to try to find out about the model in the Eatmor advertisement," said Kay. "So that hiding place will have to wait, unless Bill does some investigating."

As it happened, Bill was going to be too busy to visit the Greely mansion. Secretly Kay was pleased. She wanted to be present when the door was opened.

Midmorning of the following day found Kay and Ronald Earle heading toward Dunbar City. Ronald, glad to have Kay to himself, didn't hurry, and it was noontime before they reached the Westcott Commercial Photo Studio.

"Now to solve the mystery!" cried Kay hopefully.

She hurried upstairs to the office, Ronald following. At the photographer's Kay produced the treasured advertisement with its picture of dog and man. The studio owner instantly recognized it.

"Yes, that's one of our jobs," he acknowledged, and pointed to a large copy of the same picture, thumb-tacked to the wall.

"We would like to find the model," explained Kay.

"All I can tell you about him," answered Mr. Westcott, "is that he occasionally poses for us and photographs well. His name is Lester Lamont and he lives, let's see—where does he live?" the man asked his secretary.

The young woman went briskly to her files and reported promptly, "His address is the Dunbar City Hotel. You ought to be able to get in touch with him there."

"That's all the data we have about the man," Mr. Westcott concluded.

Thanking him, Kay and her escort raced downstairs to the car. The girl's eyes were sparkling.

"We have a real clue this time!" she triumphed. "Let's get to the hotel as fast as we can."

Ronald drove quickly to the hotel and went with Kay to the desk. Again Kay had high hopes, but they were to be dashed quickly. The hotel clerk refused to give any information whatsoever to strangers about their guests.

"Now what do we do?" asked Kay uncertainly.

"Have lunch!" suggested Ronald cheerfully. "It's after one o'clock now and I'm starved. Let's have a good meal here in the hotel to celebrate our discovery."

"There would be more to celebrate if I could find that model," replied Kay. "I'm puzzled as to—"

"Whenever you are puzzled, bewildered, or baffled, foiled or dismayed, my advice is—EAT!" Ronald teased.

"*Eatmor!*" Kay laughed finally, and allowed herself to be propelled along to the attractive dining room.

They seated themselves by a sunny window at a pleasant little table for two. The back of Kay's chair was crowded close to one behind her where a man sat alone. When he pushed back, he jostled her. Quickly he turned and apologized.

Finding Kay's reply pleasant, the man decided to join in their conversation. Ronald looked a little gloomy at this, but Kay suddenly listened closely to what the man was saying.

"I've been in the candy game all my life," he said. "Used to have a place in Denver years ago, but got cheated out of my profits there by an old skinflint. Then I opened stores in other cities and got along fairly well. I'm thinking now of going into business here in Dunbar City."

Kay heard Ronald make some polite but bored reply. She couldn't speak she was so astonished. She had recognized the talkative businessman!

"He's that angry man who came to the Greely mansion asking to see the owner," she realized.

Mr. Kane, the candy dealer, apparently did not

recognize Kay. He talked on and on. Ronald looked more and more bored and annoyed at each word.

"Are you staying at this hotel?" Ronald asked him idly, just to make conversation.

Yes, Mr. Kane was staying at the hotel. He continued talking about things he disliked in hotel life. Ronald was beginning to wish he had not spoken to him, when Kay had a sudden inspiration.

"If this man lives in the hotel, and if Lester Lamont, the Eatmor model, does too," she thought, "perhaps—!" She broke off her reflections abruptly to ask, "Mr. Kane, do you happen to know a Mr. Lamont who is staying here also?"

Ronald's bored look vanished. His eyes brightened as he realized what his companion was driving at. Mr. Kane's expression remained unchanged.

"No, I don't know the names of people here. I keep pretty much to myself."

Ronald looked completely defeated, but Kay persisted. "He's a very handsome, athletic sort of person, the movie star type, and I believe he owns a big police dog."

At mention of the animal the diner's indifferent manner changed completely. He became very excited.

"Oh, that man!" he cried. "Yes, I should say I do know him. I ought to! He had a room next to mine, and insisted on keeping that beast with him all the time. A pest and a nuisance!"

Mr. Kane was working himself into a rage very much like the one he had displayed at the mansion when speaking of the late "Skinflint" Greely.

"I complained about that man. The dog used to bark and disturb me at night! It was a nasty brute! Vicious, in fact. Growled and snapped at people in the halls and elevator. Not safe to have around! There was a big row about it."

Kay was sitting on the edge of her chair. Had she actually located the masked intruder? Could this guest with the dog and Lester Lamont be the same person?

At her first chance Kay interrupted Mr. Kane with the question, "Do you think Mr. Lamont might be in his room now?"

Ronald's eyes sparkled at the prospect of cornering the model. Mr. Kane's answer, however, was disappointing.

"Oh, no. Lamont, if that's his name, isn't here anymore. There were so many complaints about his dog the management asked him to leave."

Mr. Kane mentioned this fact casually. He had no idea how deflating his words were to the two young detectives!

"To think we almost had him and then he eluded us again!" said Kay to herself. Aloud, she asked, "I don't suppose you know where he went?"

To her surprise Mr. Kane replied, "Oh, yes. I believe he went to a town some distance from here, a place called Brantwood."

XIII

Another Discovery

The candy man, seeing that the young people were interested in his reference to the town they lived in, went on with his conversation.

"When I heard that fellow say he was leaving for Brantwood I mentioned to him that I had been there myself," he said. "I told him I had gone to see a person by the name of Manuel Greely and found that he had died."

Ronald and Kay exchanged glances at this reference, but said nothing. The man continued:

"This Lamont then said he knew all about Greely and the mansion."

This time Kay and Ronald avoided each other's eyes, so that Mr. Kane wouldn't suspect from their looks that they were very excited over the information. The man now devoted himself to his dinner.

"Let's hurry home. I want to tell Bill about this," whispered Kay, leaning across the table and speaking to Ronald.

"Can't we stop at the movies?" Ronald suggested. "You promised to spend the day with me," he said obstinately. "An hour or so more won't make any difference. You can't say no to a picture named *The Haunted House!*"

Kay gave in on the promise that they would stop at the Greely house on their way back. "I want to see if that police dog's owner showed up, and if so, what he looks like," she said.

It was late afternoon when they began the drive to Brantwood. Kay, with her mind on the mystery, was startled to hear her companion say, "How about stopping some place for supper?"

"Oh, Ronald, you can't possibly be hungry again!" Kay exclaimed.

"Yes, I am," replied Ronald. "Come on, here's a nice little restaurant!" In spite of Kay's protests he stopped his automobile. "Not a word of criticism about my appetite," he warned. "Remember, if I hadn't insisted on lunch you wouldn't have found out about Lamont from *Candy Kane!*"

Kay laughed, then suddenly became serious as she saw a police car stop another car and the officer pull out a pad of summons slips.

"What bad luck!" Kay said sympathetically. "It's Chris Eaton. The horse smashed her headlight and now she's getting a ticket for improper lights!"

"No matter what broke it, the officer isn't as impressed with her charm as Cody was!" Ronald laughed wickedly. "I wonder why she's not parading around in her new outfit?" he said.

"Chris looks pretty in her regular clothes," said Kay, determined to say something good about the girl.

"She doesn't look nearly as beautiful as somebody else I know!" declared Ronald. "Well, come on, let's eat."

It was very dark by the time the couple reached the Greely mansion, but they found the house and the stables in a blaze of light.

"Something must have happened," said Kay, worried, as Ronald stopped the car.

Something had happened, but it was quite different from what the girl might have guessed. She learned from Tom that no one had been detected around the grounds. The police dog had not been seen again. It was assumed either that it had come there in the first place without its owner, or that its master, if he were spying on the property, had not gone near the house.

"But that Mr. Cody hasn't come back," said Tom. "Jimmy is pretty worried about him."

"You mean he hasn't been here since he went after the runaway horse yesterday?" Kay cried.

"That's right," replied Curran.

Excitedly Kay ran to the barn and sought out Jimmy. The groom told the same story. "Mr. Cody's hoss didn't come back, either," he drawled. "Sometimes if a rider falls off, his pony will return without him."

"Of course it's as unfamiliar with the surroundings as its master is," said Kay.

"But lots o' times a hoss has got more sense about direction than a human has," replied Jimmy. "I dunno what to do. I'm sure Mr. Cody's had an accident."

Kay agreed, and promised to do something about hunting for the missing man. She and Ronald drove to the Tracey home as fast as they dared, and reported the news to Bill.

"This is serious," the lawyer decided, going at once to the telephone. "I'll notify the police and get them to send out a search party. If they find no sign of Cody tonight we'll organize another search party early tomorrow to carry on the hunt. Want to come, Ronald?"

"Try to keep me away!" was his quick reply. "I'll be over here at dawn if you say so."

After he had left, Kay telephoned the Worth twins

to find out how Wendy was feeling, and to tell them about the latest happening at the Greely estate.

"I'm fine again," said Wendy, who answered the call. When she heard about Cody's disappearance, she asked fearfully, "Do you think the masked stranger could have been in the woods and harmed him?"

Kay hadn't thought of this, though she had to admit the theory was worth considering. Wendy asked if she could help them the next day; Betty wouldn't be able to go.

"Yes of course," invited Kay. "We'll pick you up. Be ready early."

At five o'clock the following morning Bill Tracey telephoned to police headquarters. As soon as he learned that no trace of Clarence Cody had been found, he awoke Kay. She dressed in a jiffy, and together the cousins prepared a quick breakfast. Wendy and Ronald were ready when the two stopped for them, both eager to help solve this new mystery.

"Here come some troopers out of the woods," said Kay, as Bill stopped in the Greely driveway. "Mr. Cody isn't with them."

The men told how they had tramped all night through woods and thickets, mud and briars, and over rocks. They looked tired and dishevelled. There was no trace of the lost rancher anywhere.

A fresh squad of troopers had just come, carrying first aid kits and ropes for use in case of emergency. Everyone felt that some serious accident had occurred to prevent Cody's return.

"I'd like to take a horse and ride out on the search with Jimmy and you, Mr. Tracey," Tom Curran offered. "That is, if Miss Tracey here and her friends will guard the place while I'm gone."

"Aw, say yes," pleaded Jimmy. "He knows his way

around these woods, and that's more than I do, or poor Mr. Cody either."

Secretly Ronald would have liked the adventure, yet he wanted to do whatever might be most helpful.

"We'll stay!" Kay offered, telling herself this would be a good time to continue exploring the mansion.

The search party started off. It had been arranged that the police scouts would go North and scout the woods in that direction on foot. Bill and Jimmy were to hunt on horseback toward the South. Tom Curran, also mounted, took the middle or Western area of the wooded mountain that stretched for miles behind the estate.

As the groups departed, Kay said, "Ronald, come upstairs with us and we'll show you the sealed door in the hall. Wendy, you're not afraid of it anymore, are you?" she smiled.

"No," the girl replied, "only I think we should be careful."

They went up the steps, on the alert for any lurking intruder. Kay led the way to the mysterious door. Ronald and the two girls pushed against it, since it had no knob. Their combined efforts failed to move or break the wood.

"Maybe it's just a dummy," said Kay.

"No, I don't think so," said Ronald, knocking on the wall. "It sounds hollow. Maybe there's some other way of getting into the room or closet it leads to."

"How?" Wendy asked.

"Let's try the room on the other side of the wall," urged Kay. "It used to be the master bedroom," she explained to Ronald.

The spot behind the door proved to be a partition covered with flowered paper. This was torn away easily.

"Here it is!" Kay cried excitedly as another entrance was revealed.

"And this one opens!" added Ronald, swinging it wide.

The young detectives peered behind it. A good-sized space was discovered between the walls. It was, in fact, a sort of little room.

"It's very dark in here," Wendy remarked.

"I'll get my flashlight," Ronald offered, hurrying to his car for it.

In a few minutes the dim interior of the secret chamber was lighted up by Ronald's flashlight.

"Nothing in here but a kind of bureau," he reported.

Kay stepped in farther. "It isn't a bureau," she said, examining something in one corner. "It's a filing cabinet."

"So it is!" agreed the boy, aiming his flashlight on the object. "Metal and fireproof. It may hold some important papers."

Kay pulled out the drawers and found an assortment of business papers and documents.

"We can't read these in this dark cubbyhole," objected Ronald. "Let's pull the whole thing into the other room."

"Do you think we can? It's very heavy," said Wendy.

"Let me try!" said Ronald, rolling up his sleeves and showing his muscular arms.

He caught hold of a corner of the cabinet and strained to move it. Although his arms bulged and his face turned red with the effort, he succeeded in edging it along only a few inches.

"We'll help you," said Kay, propping up the flashlight where it would shine in the dark compartment.

"All right," said Ronald. "Now then, one, two, THREE!"

Together the young people struggled with all their might. The file was moved again a few inches nearer the door.

"Once more!" Ronald encouraged. Again he counted, "One, two, three, HEAVE!"

This time the heavy load scraped against the wall.

"O-o-o-w!" screamed Kay shrilly.

"What's the matter?" Ronald and Wendy asked in unison.

"My finger! Ouch!" Kay yelped in pain. "It's jammed between the wall and the cabinet, and o-o-o-o-h, how it hurts!"

"I'll try to move this thing and you pull your hand out!" Ronald instructed.

He and Wendy could not budge the heavy case.

"What are we going to do?" Wendy asked fearfully, seeing the look of pain on Kay's face.

"I'll get the tire iron from my car," said Ronald quickly, hurrying off.

As the boy left the room, there was a terrific crash on the first floor!

XIV

Surprises!

There was a resounding smash and the tinkle of shattered glass. Then silence. Ronald raced down the stairs.

"Go and see what it is!" Kay urged Wendy.

"I don't want to leave you stuck like this!" her friend objected.

"You've got to!" insisted Kay. "My finger's so numb now anyway it doesn't even hurt anymore. Ronald may need you."

Wendy made her way to the first floor. She fully expected to come face to face with the masked intruder.

In the meantime Ronald had reached the main hall and was looking around corners cautiously. Now he stood in one of the front rooms, where the cause of the crash was evident. A window had been smashed. Scattered across the floor were the pieces of the broken pane.

Before Ronald could investigate, something struck him across the face! The blow came from a large, soft object that made a strange whirring sound.

Ronald's eyes blinked shut as they were struck with a thud. Instantly he put both hands across his face, and dodged, but no second blow came.

When he looked up, there was nothing to be seen.

He had almost decided that the place was haunted, when something flew toward him again.

"A wild pheasant!" Ronald gasped in relief as the bird passed him.

Wendy rushed up. "I'm glad it wasn't a burglar," she gasped.

Leaving the room, Ronald hurried outside to get the tool from the car, while Wendy quickly raised the broken window sash.

"Now you can find your way out, my fine feathered friend!" she spoke invitingly.

Ronald returned quickly, and he and Wendy went upstairs to release Kay.

"A pheasant!" exclaimed the latter in amazement, when her friend reported on the identity of the housebreaker. "It must have been frightened badly by something."

"Maybe that police dog is back or the masked man," murmured Wendy.

"As soon as I can get away from this spot, I'm going to find out," said Kay determinedly.

Meanwhile, Ronald opened a kit of tools. Using the tire iron as a lever, he was able to move the cabinet enough to release Kay's finger.

"Oh, what a relief!" the girl cried gratefully.

Her friends wanted her to do something about the injury but she assured them the returning circulation would take care of it. She was more interested in investigating the cause of the pheasant's fright.

While this had been going on, a figure had crawled like a shadow through the shrubbery and reached the house. He saw the open window and went to peer in. At that very moment the bird flew out! Its plump feathery body whacked the man in the nose, knocking off his mask. His exclamation of surprise and the scuffle that followed as he thrashed back at the bird were plainly audible to those above.

Kay raced to a window and arrived just in time to see a fleeing figure vanish into the woods. She did not see the man's face, so she could not identify him, but she was sure he was the former intruder.

"We never could catch him now," said Ronald.

"We'd better board up that broken window!" Kay suggested.

Ronald went off in search of boards and nails. "There's somebody knocking!" he called from the hall.

Kay and Wendy hurried to the kitchen door to see a state trooper standing there.

"Have you had news yet of the missing rider from any of the searchers?" the officer inquired.

"No, not a word," Kay answered anxiously. "Have you?"

"We haven't found anything, either," the man replied. "We'll keep in touch with this place from time to time. We can call in the other scouts and all of us go to help the rescuers if necessary."

"From Friday to Sunday is a long time to be lost," Kay noted in a worried manner.

"Yes, it looks as if Mr. Cody may have been in an accident," said the trooper, shaking his head in a discouraged way.

The officer went off to continue the search, while Kay and her friends, after nailing up the broken window, resumed their inspection of the cabinet. Its contents, which were brought into the bedroom for examination, seemed disappointing at first.

"Nothing but old papers!" grumbled Ronald. "No shining gold or glittering jewels!"

Kay, who was examining the "old papers" carefully, suddenly gave a little cry of excitement.

"This may prove to be more valuable than we thought," she said.

"Why, what is it?" asked Ronald, peering over the girl's shoulder with curiosity.

"Here is a bundle of deeds to several pieces of property," Kay explained. "See, this one proves the ownership of this estate."

"Everybody knew old Greely owned this place anyhow," said Wendy, unimpressed.

"Yes, but this is the legal proof, and besides, look at the other deeds here. Mr. Greely owned lots of real estate."

"Ha, ha!" chortled Ronald, picking out a bundle of typewritten sheets fastened with red tape. "Look here! The actual deed to Candy Kane's place in Denver."

"This will make everything much easier for Cousin Bill to settle," Kay remarked. "Here are listings of some oil wells in Oklahoma! I wonder if they are valuable?"

"They may have gone dry by now," commented Wendy.

"And here are bank books. Just look at the amount of money in them!" gasped Kay.

Ronald gaped at the surprising figures. "I don't believe it! There isn't that much money in the world!" he sighed comically. "Surely Mr. Greely drew out and spent most of it before he died!"

"Bill will have to investigate this," said Kay. "Why, the old man had money saved in banks as well as a fortune concealed about this house."

"Suppose this mansion had burned down!" exclaimed Wendy.

"That would have been terrible for Peter Greely," remarked Kay.

"Peter Greely? Who's he?" asked Ronald. "Is he young as well as rich?"

"He's about twenty-seven," replied Kay, "but he doesn't know he's rich!"

"You mean he doesn't know he has a fortune?" gasped the boy.

"He thinks he's poor!" laughed Kay. "What a surprise for him! He's an airplane pilot and believes this property isn't worth much."

"Where is he now?" Ronald asked.

"He has flown to England on some kind of a secret mission for the government in regard, I believe, to airplanes."

"Well," reflected Ronald, "if he doesn't fall out of the clouds from an airplane, the shock of finding all this unexpected wealth on his hands when he gets down to earth will make him collapse, I bet. It would me!"

"No wonder that masked man keeps trying to break in here," said Kay. "He must know what the old house contains!"

"We'd better stuff all these papers back in the cabinet and hide it again until your cousin can take charge of it," advised Ronald soberly. He went to work briskly.

"I wonder where Bill is?" Kay said uneasily. "I guess he hasn't been successful in his search."

The early morning sun had risen high in the clear blue sky. Ronald did not need to look at it to guess the hour, however.

"I know it's lunch time!" he declared. "My stomach tells me so!"

"I never knew an alarm clock like your appetite!" laughed Kay.

At that moment the three young people heard the sound of horses' hoofs. Some of the searchers were returning.

"Bill's here," cried Kay looking out of a window, "and Jimmy's with him."

She turned and ran downstairs to speak to the men. In response to her first question, Bill answered soberly: "No. Not a trace of Cody. He can't be found."

This bad news dampened the spirits of everyone. Jimmy was in the depths of despair about the fate of his employer. He stumped off dismally to feed the horses in the stable.

"We'll help you!" offered Kay in a desire to comfort the stableman.

She and her friends began doling out a portion of corn to each animal. In turn the horses whinnied eagerly and thrust out their soft noses.

"I love horses," said Kay, patting those she fed.

Ronald, too, was enjoying the job. Jimmy, however, hurried along morosely, thinking only of how soon he could get back on the trail to search for the lost ranchman. He moved quickly from stall to stall until he reached the last one. Then he let out a roar.

"Brownie's gone! Somebody's stolen a horse!" he yelled.

XV

Strange Visitor

At Jimmy's cry of alarm, Kay and Ronald raced to the rear of the stable. There was Brownie's place, still bedded with straw. Jimmy stood beside it, holding the horse's share of corn. But the stall was empty!

"Perhaps the masked man stole him!" flashed through Kay's mind, though she did not mention this idea in front of Jimmy. "Maybe he's just broken loose," she suggested aloud.

"He couldn't have," said Jimmy. "He was tied fast. See, the rope's gone!"

"Couldn't it have come undone?" asked Ronald.

"Not the way I tied it," answered Jimmy grimly. "No, somebody's been here and—"

His words were drowned by the roar of a car, whose engine was being raced by a bad driver.

"Maybe they've found Mr. Cody!" cried Kay hopefully.

Jimmy stumbled past the others in his eagerness to find out. Ronald, Wendy, and Kay followed. It was only Chris Eaton.

Ronald groaned and looked away. The stableman grunted and busied himself looking for some trace of the lost animal.

"Where is Mr. Cody?" inquired Chris haughtily.

"Haven't you heard?" asked Kay in surprise. "He's

been lost on the mountain ever since Friday night. Searchers are out hunting for him."

Chris gave a little shriek. "What do you mean?" she gasped, pressing her hands to her head in a great show of shock and dismay.

"I mean just what I say," replied Kay. "He went off to catch a runaway horse and hasn't been seen since. We're afraid he's had an accident."

At this Chris screamed hysterically. "Oh, oh, how terrible! Why aren't you people doing something? Why are you just standing around when maybe he's lying hurt out there in those woods! And why is Jimmy loafing here when he should be out searching?"

"You're putting on quite an act!" remarked Ronald coldly, and walked away with Kay and Wendy.

Chris now burst into uncontrollable sobbing, wringing her hands and scolding, "Haven't any of you any feelings? Somebody do something!"

As they ignored Chris, she besieged Jimmy with tearful questions.

"Don't come around here botherin' me!" the little man snapped.

"But won't you do anything to help?" the girl wailed.

Jimmy turned on her irritably. "You go on and get outa here!" he ordered. "I got troubles enough without you. Go on, get out!" he commanded angrily.

Insulted, Chris ran off to question the others. They had disappeared, so she drove away.

Kay had told Bill about the discovery of the valuable legal papers in the cabinet, so they, together with Wendy and Ronald, had gone upstairs so the lawyer could examine the documents.

"These are amazing!" he declared. "Of course, it's impossible to compute the total value of Greely's holdings yet, but the total amount of his estate will be astounding. His greatnephew will undoubtedly be a millionaire!"

The subject was discussed further as the girls raided Curran's supplies and fixed up a lunch. Kay was a good cook, and in a short time she and Wendy were serving a delicious meal in the big, old-fashioned kitchen. Bill and Ronald ate hungrily, while Wendy carried a plateful of food to the quarters over the stable where Jimmy was living.

"You're amazing, Kay," praised Ronald, his mouth full of potatoes. "A detective one minute and a cook the next."

He finished eating before the others did and said he would like to continue the treasure hunt.

"I'm going upstairs to that secret room," he stated. "I have an idea the space may extend farther back between those walls than we thought it would. There may be more of the fortune hidden in some dark corner."

"Go ahead!" urged Kay. "I'll join you as soon as I finish this apple."

Ronald returned to the cubbyhole and felt his way inside. Flashlight in hand, he had gone along for six feet or more beyond the cabinet without finding anything, when his battery went dead.

"What a pain!" fumed Ronald. "Well, maybe I can feel my way along somehow."

In utter blackness he shuffled forward.

"I hope I don't crack my knees on another filing cabinet," he thought.

No sooner had this idea passed through his mind than his feet reached an opening in the floor. Down he shot; down, down, through space and inky darkness. It seemed to be a bottomless pit!

If this gap had a bottom, and if Ronald made a thump when he hit it, nobody knew, for just at that moment there came a thunderous knock on the kitchen door. Bill opened it to find a roughly dressed man standing there. The caller was a complete stranger to him.

"What can I do for you?" Bill asked, then wondered whether the man might be some farmer who had news of Cody.

"I came to see Mr. Manuel Greely," said the man. "I hope he's well."

"I'm very sorry, but Mr. Greely passed away some time ago," Bill answered, studying the newcomer.

The stranger looked genuinely distressed. "I'm mighty sorry to hear that!" he said in friendly concern. "Mighty, mighty sorry!"

The expression on his frank, open face showed that he was sincere in his remark. The man, though dressed poorly, was plainly neither a loafer nor a tramp. His clothes had the knockabout look of much usage out-of-doors. His friendly face was suntanned and deeply weather-beaten. His hands were tough and callused. The Traceys wondered who he could be, and what his connection might have been with the eccentric Mr. Greely.

"Won't you come in?" Kay invited.

"Is there anything we can do for you?" Bill added.

"Well, thank you, I'll sit down a minute," the man accepted gratefully. "I've had a long walk and my legs aren't as spry as they used to be!"

He settled himself rather stiffly in a chair. Then he unbuttoned his coat.

"My name's Mulligan," he explained, "Martin Mulligan. I'm a fisherman by trade, and old Mr. Greely used to like to go out to sea on fishing trips with me. Yes, we went many a time!"

Kay now realized that the man's tanned face had the look of a sailor who had braved the winds and the sea. His rocking gait, too, was the personification of "sea-legs" ashore.

"Old Mr. Greely and I had numerous fine outings together," the seaman reminisced. "I'm sorry to hear he's gone." Martin Mulligan shook his grisled head regretfully.

"The idea of Manuel Greely being a sportsman is a new one to us," Bill commented. "We think of him only as a businessman."

"Well, yes, I guess Mr. Greely was plenty smart about making money," the caller replied. "Anyway, he always bought the most expensive fishing tackle. He was a good sport, and we had some regular adventures together!"

"Adventures?" asked Kay eagerly.

"Yes, ma'am. He was a smart one about finding out things, I can tell you. Sometimes I think he knew more about the sea than I do. I recall one time he was fishing and we spied some kind of yellow-gray stuff floating on the ocean. Kind of a wax it was. He made me heave to and collect all that stuff and take it ashore. I'd have left it to float away!"

"Was it ambergris?" asked Kay excitedly, remembering her experience in the perfume factory.

"That's what old Mr. Greely thought it was," answered the fisherman. "To tell the truth, that's why I'm here. I been runnin' into bad luck the past year and been pretty hard up. I thought if that stuff *was* ambergris, I had a right to share in it because I helped him collect it."

"I haven't heard that Mr. Greely had any of it," Bill responded.

Kay suddenly wondered if one of those intriguing red "X" marks on the map which the masked man had stolen might tell where the ambergris lay hidden.

"I hoped to get a little money for it," sighed the

fisherman sadly, "but I guess I'm just out of luck again."

"It's too bad you've made the trip out here for nothing," said Kay sympathetically. "Won't you have a cup of coffee and some sandwiches before you go?"

The seaman beamed. "I'd sure like to," he said, grinning broadly. "To tell the truth," he added, "I've got to find work of some kind to do. Without Mr. Greely to fall back on, I'm lost!"

After further conversation Bill Tracey was convinced that the visitor was to be trusted. He offered Mulligan the job of handyman about the place to help Curran.

"That's next best to being with Mr. Greely himself," Mulligan said. "We were good friends and you can depend on it, I'll guard his interests while I'm here!"

Certain that the seaman was an ideal employee for the estate, Bill took him out to look over the grounds and to arrange for his duties and living quarters. Wendy, saying she would wash the dishes, insisted that Kay go upstairs and help Ronald in his search for treasure.

"I'd forgotten all about him!" Kay said. "I can't imagine what he's been doing all this time."

At the moment she spoke a trooper stamped up on the porch and called out, "We've found Mr. Cody's horse!"

"Which one did you find?" asked Kay.

"Not the runaway," replied the policeman. "We caught his saddle horse. I guess Cody's making his way out of the woods on foot."

"If he isn't lying on the ground somewhere with a broken leg," remarked Bill, who had come up to hear the announcement.

"They're still looking for him, and they may find him yet," the trooper stated encouragingly.

Since Kay could do nothing about the search for the missing man, she decided to hurry upstairs to the secret room and find out what Ronald might have discovered.

"Ron-ald!" she called loudly.

No answer. Kay called again and hesitated at the cubbyhole. "Maybe he found a secret passageway in the wall." This idea appealed to her imagination so much that she entered the nook and fumbled along it, shouting "Ron-ald! Ron-ald!"

She was following in his footsteps through the darkness. Unsuspectingly she approached the same treacherous opening he had. In another second her feet felt nothing under them. Down she fell through space as Ronald had done. Down, down she whirled into the same bottomless pit!

XVI

The Twins' Clue

Kay fell from the second floor to the basement. She slid all the way at breakneck speed down a smooth incline. Reaching the end, the girl shot out onto the floor, right on top of Ronald Earle.

Ronald lay stretched out, completely unconscious. As Kay gathered her bearings and sat up, she realized that he was probably hurt.

"He must have hit the concrete hard," Kay thought in alarm. "Poor Ronald! He broke my fall. Oh, I hope I didn't break any of his bones."

A glance at the opening through which she had fallen showed her what it was—merely a laundry chute!

"Ronald! Ronald!" Kay called, rubbing his limp hands vigorously.

Ronald made no response. Kay now shouted desperately for her cousin, but there was no answer. Deep in the cavernous basement, the girl's cries were muffled by the thick stone walls. She was about to go limping upstairs to get help, when Ronald opened his eyes and stared at her in a blank, dazed way.

"What happened?" he murmured feebly.

"You fell," said Kay. "Can you move?"

"Not very well!" Ronald groaned, sore with bruises.

Kay lifted her voice again and yelled for Cousin

Bill. Ronald, gingerly sitting up, called too. This time there was some response. Martin Mulligan, the new handyman, first to hear the commotion in the lower region, muttered to himself:

"There must be ghosts down there!"

He called Bill, who switched on the basement lights, and the two men went to investigate the noise.

"How in the world did you get down here?" the lawyer asked as he stared in amazement at the dishevelled couple on the floor.

Ronald rose uncertainly to his shaky legs and rubbed his head. A lump on his forehead was rapidly turning an ugly greenish-blue.

"What a black eye you're going to have!" observed Mulligan. "What happened?"

"I don't know yet!" answered Ronald, still dazed.

"We came down in the express elevator!" Kay said, pointing to the laundry chute. "We fell into it through that dark passage on the second floor."

"Are you all right?" asked Bill, examining the two victims anxiously.

"I guess this house is full of all sorts of crazy things," commented Mulligan. "I recall the old man telling me of some of them. Have you ever seen his trophy room?"

"Trophy room?" asked Kay. "No, that's something we've missed."

"There is one here some place. I remember Mr. Greely mentioned it once. We were out all day. He was real tickled with a big fish he caught and said he was going to have it stuffed to hang on the wall of his trophy room. Said he liked hunting, too, and had some heads of big game mounted."

"We ought to look for it!" cried Kay, excited. "Just think, after all our exploring there's another spot we've never found!"

"We've never searched the basement," said Bill.

"Let's look now while we're here!" Kay begged. "Do you feel like you can, Ronald?"

"Oh, yes, I'm okay!" Ronald replied, holding one hand to his forehead. "If you are going to find any more secret passageways don't leave me out. I wouldn't want to miss anything!"

Ronald insisted upon joining the hunt. An examination of the laundry and vast furnace room revealed nothing at first.

"This place is so big and has so many nooks and crannies that it's a real chore to look in them all," Bill declared in despair.

"Here's something!" called Kay, poking her head into what appeared to be a cold cellar for jams and jellies. "This closet looks like it might be a false front for a room hidden behind it."

Bill, Ronald, and Mulligan quickly went to investigate Kay's discovery. Sure enough, on the back wall of the closet was the outline of a door.

"Sealed shut," said Ronald in disgust.

"Let me get at it," said Mulligan.

The sailor's strong hands soon loosened a panel. It came out, revealing a long dark passage ahead.

"Whew, what a damp, musty smell," sniffed Kay.

"I'll go in first. You folks follow," said Mulligan staunchly.

The search party went forward, single file.

"Another locked door!" announced the leader, coming to the end of the narrow passage and wrestling with a rusty padlock.

"What a house!" said Ronald. "Tunnels and everything! It's like an old castle with dungeons!"

"I've got the lock loose!" announced Mulligan.

The door creaked open and the eager party of explorers looked through. Only a yawning cave of darkness faced them. Bill lit a match. Its tiny flicker had scarcely pierced the blackness of the subcellar when it went out.

"I don't have another match," he said, feeling in all his pockets.

"That's okay. I've found the electric switch," Mulligan called out.

He clicked the button hopefully, but the light did not turn on. Then he found a single match in his own pocket, but when he scratched it, the head snapped off!

"We can't stay here any longer," Bill said. "We'll come back later with flashlights. We should go upstairs now and see whether there is any word of Cody."

The disappointed group filed through the damp and musty passageway. A shout at the kitchen door announced the return of Tom Curran. He was leading the runaway Queenie.

"She's survived her adventure," he reported, "but where her master is, nobody knows!"

Jimmy came to take the horse and also the mud-splashed weary animal which Tom had ridden. He was very worried about the long disappearance of the rancher.

The Traceys and their friends, too, were downhearted at the failure of the search party to find the missing man. Since there was nothing more they could do, however, they returned to Brantwood. As they ate dinner Kay, her cousin, and her mother discussed the status of the mystery.

"We don't seem to be solving it very fast," sighed Kay. "I feel that if we could only locate the masked man, we'd learn a lot."

"I'd certainly like to get back the plans of the house and see where those 'X' marks are," said Bill grimly.

"But that wouldn't help locate Mr. Cody," said Mrs. Tracey.

"I'm not entirely sure it wouldn't," Kay disagreed. "We think it was his police dog that chased Queenie, so Mr. Cody may have met the man in the woods. There's no telling what might have happened then."

"It does seem strange that after all this time not one of the searchers has any clue to Mr. Cody, if he's still on the mountainside," agreed Kay's mother.

The solution of any part of the mystery remained at a standstill until the next morning, when Kay met Betty and Wendy at school. Mrs. Tracey had driven her to Carmont, so she had not taken the train she usually rode with them. Excited, they rushed up to their friend when they saw her.

"You'll never guess who was at the Brantwood station this morning!" they cried in chorus.

"If I can't guess, you'd better tell me," Kay answered, smiling.

"You remember that woman we saw at the mansion of secrets, the first time we went there?" asked Betty.

"The one who pried open the seventh step looking for something?" asked Kay.

"Yes, that's right!" chorused the twins.

"She was buying a ticket," reported Betty.

"A ticket to where?" asked Kay.

"Oh, Kay, you always think of everything," sighed Wendy. "I wish we were as clever. It never occurred to us to find out."

"Well, maybe we still can," said Kay hopefully. "We'll check on our way home."

Fortunately the ticket agent was able to give the girls the information they wanted. The woman had purchased a ticket to Dunbar City.

"Your clue is wonderful!" Kay congratulated the twins enthusiastically. "I wish I could go to Dunbar City right now and look for the mysterious woman, but I have something else to do. We'll do that later. But the first thing to do is to find Mr. Cody. Let's go up on the mountaintop and take Bill's binoculars along. We might catch a long distance glimpse of the missing man somewhere in those hills!"

"We could get lost in the woods ourselves," objected Wendy.

"No chance of that. I know a safe, clear trail to the top," said Kay reassuringly.

Kay got the family car and drove with Wendy and Betty to a spot where a footpath led directly up the mountain. She parked the automobile and led the way through the woods.

"It's a wonderful lookout!" said Kay, scrambling up the steep, rocky hillside. "You can see miles of countryside."

The view was beautiful. Betty was enthusiastic about the spreading landscape, while Wendy could not suppress a poetic outburst. Kay pulled out Bill's binoculars and began adjusting them to her vision.

"This is wonderful!" she said. "Everything stands out so clearly! What's that noise?" she asked suddenly, putting down the instrument.

There was the sound of a crash through the bushes behind them. Was someone coming?

"O-o-o-h! Look!" cried Wendy, frightened.

There stood a huge buck deer. The animal paused in a moment of astonishment. Then it lowered its great, branching antlers and shook them threateningly! Wendy gave a cry of terror and darted behind a rock for safety. Betty began to climb a tree! Kay, who thought deer were timid creatures, waved her arms and shouted sharply:

"Shoo! Go 'way!"

The buck evidently was as afraid of the girls as they were of him. When Kay called and motioned, it merely raised its head, then ran off.

She adjusted the binoculars again and looked around. There was not a sign of Clarence Cody, a horse, or of anyone else.

"Of course, I can't see through the leaves," Kay joked. Then she added seriously, "Let's do a little scouting on the way back to the car."

As they made their descent, the friends peered behind every tree and under each bush within a radius of a hundred feet of the path. Not one single clue rewarded their search. About halfway to the foot of the mountain Wendy halted and called to her companions.

"Listen!" she said. "I hear that animal again!"

There certainly was the sound of something moving through the foliage. In another moment a figure appeared. It was not that of the deer, but of a woodsman. He had a good-natured face, and was swinging along with an ax over one shoulder. He nodded pleasantly.

"On a hike?" he asked with a smile.

"We've been trying to find a man who got lost in these hills," explained Kay.

"A man who got lost?" inquired the newcomer with interest. "What did he look like?"

"He wore a red plaid flannel shirt, riding breeches, and high leather boots," Kay said, describing Cody.

"I saw him!" the woodsman exclaimed.

XVII

The Trophy Room

Kay and the Worth twins hung on the words of the woodsman, who had seen the missing Clarence Cody.

"I met him in the forest not long ago," he informed them. "He asked me how to get back to the old Greely place near Brantwood."

"Was he injured?" Kay asked.

"No, but he looked pretty tired and dirty."

"He has been out several nights," Kay answered. "Can you give us any idea where he is now so we can try to find him and drive him home?"

"Well, let's see," said the man, setting down his ax and scratching his head reflectively. "I met him a couple of miles beyond here on what we call the Birch Trail. I told him to follow it and branch off on a path he'd come to by a spring. If he does that, he ought to come out on Route 33 near Hopper's roadstand. You might meet him there."

"We'll try it," said Kay. "You've been a great help. Thank you!"

"Not at all. Glad to be of assistance," answered the woodsman, lifting his ax to his shoulder again and striding along through the trees.

The three girls hurried excitedly down the remainder of the trail to the parked car.

"I'm so glad he's alive," said Wendy.

"And not injured," added Kay. "But why has he been gone so long? Well, we'll soon find out."

Reaching the automobile, she asked Wendy and Betty to get in quickly. "We have a long drive to Hopper's roadstand and we don't want to miss Mr. Cody."

"That's right," Betty replied, "and you should have the honor of bringing in the lost man, Kay."

"You two have to share the credit if we find him," her friend insisted.

The three companions rode along eagerly, following the woodsman's directions. They circled around the foot of the mountain and finally came out on a white flat ribbon of concrete road. Kay increased her speed. High wooded cliffs bordered one side of the highway, while the other broke off into ravines.

"I hope Mr. Cody doesn't fall over a cliff," worried Wendy, looking up at the rocky wall above her.

"Wouldn't it be great if we actually did head him off where the woodland path meets this highway?" said Betty.

"Hopper's roadstand ought to be somewhere along here," Kay said.

Presently a small building loomed up before them, nestling at the foot of the cliff.

"The trail should come out just beyond here," said the twins' friend. "Keep a sharp lookout."

As the car cruised along slowly, Betty suddenly exclaimed, "There's a man ahead of us. He's just coming out of the woods!"

"He's wearing a red shirt!" cried Kay excitedly, speeding up.

"And riding breeches!" shouted Wendy.

The man was hesitating by the roadside, evidently uncertain which direction he should take.

"Mr. Cody! Mr. Cody!" shouted Kay, stopping her car and waving to him frantically.

A smile lit up the man's haggard and unshaven face. "Can I believe my eyes!" he answered, stepping quickly to the car. "I sure am glad to see familiar folks!"

"We're certainly happy to see you!" Kay responded. "Get in the car and we'll drive you home."

"A whole crowd of men and boys and a squad of state troopers have been out searching for you!" said Betty.

"What happened?" asked Wendy anxiously. "Were you hurt?"

"Yes, I was," admitted the man, easing himself gingerly into the car. He sank back on the seat, his face chalk white under the black stubble of his three-day-old beard. "My horse was frightened by that same police dog that chased Queenie. It bolted, stumbled, and threw me over a cliff."

"I was afraid you'd fall over one," said Wendy.

"Well, I sure did. Knocked me out completely. When I came to, the dog and both horses were gone. It was pitch dark. I spent the night in a cave I found. The next day I felt too shaken up to move very much. I thought it best to take it easy for a while, so I camped out until I felt better."

"How did you manage without food?" asked Wendy.

"Don't worry about a Westerner starving in the woods," smiled the rancher. "I made a slingshot of an elastic band I found in my pocket and a forked stick cut from a tree. I killed a rabbit and roasted it over a little fire. There were plenty of wild berries and a spring nearby, so I didn't starve."

"I'm surprised none of the searchers saw the smoke," said Betty.

"I was down below where they probably were looking," replied Cody; "in fact, I couldn't climb up the cliff so I tried to crawl through a tunnel."

"That's why you didn't hear the men calling," speculated Kay. "Did you get out that way?"

"Yes, I did," Cody replied. "Then I got my sense of direction by the sun and walked through the woods. After a while I met a man who told me which way to reach the highway."

"We met him, too, and he directed us to the path you took."

"All's well that ends well," said the rancher. "But I'm sorry I lost the horses."

"They've been found and are safe in the stable," Kay cheered the man.

As they rode along, the girls wondered if they should tell him about the stolen horse, but decided to wait. One thing was certain: if the masked man had taken the animal to trail Cody, he had not been successful. Who had stolen Brownie, and why, remained as much of a mystery as ever.

"Here we are at Brantwood!" cried Betty presently. "Stop at our house; it's the nearest."

"I'll phone to the police that you've been found, Mr. Cody," said Kay. "And I must call Bill right away!"

In response to this welcome telephone message, Bill drove immediately to the Worth house. He found the rancher enjoying a meal of chicken sandwiches and milk. Mr. Cody, after thanking the girls, was driven to the Greely estate by Bill Tracey.

The news of the missing man's return got a front page headline in the morning paper. Chris Eaton read this and appeared at school in her cowgirl outfit.

"I'm going to have my first riding lesson this afternoon," she informed everyone as she strutted about.

"It was pretty smart of Kay and the twins to find Cody!" remarked Ronald.

"He was found by a woodsman who lives in those hills. Those girls had nothing to do with it!" sniffed Chris.

"She's just heartbroken because she didn't rescue him herself!" said one of Kay's friends later when she heard the remark.

After school Chris Eaton hurried out to the Greely place, to find that Kay and Ronald had reached there ahead of her. She paid no attention to them.

While Chris was sauntering to the stables, the other two hurried indoors. Both were eager to continue their search of the basement passageways.

"I have a new flashlight battery this time," said Ronald, "and a kit of tools besides, so we can fix that electric light. Have you a new bulb to screw in there?"

"Yes, right here."

The explorers followed the underground tunnel until they reached the room that had been discovered before. Ronald swept the darkness with his flash. Kay gasped at the sight it revealed, and for one second thought the buck from the mountain was about to charge upon her! Glaring down upon the couple from every wall were heads of wild animals, many of them ferocious looking in the dim light.

"We've found the trophy room!" cried Kay. "These must be the mounted heads of big game that Martin Mulligan told us about!"

Ronald quickly repaired the electric switch. Then Kay screwed in the new bulb and snapped on the light.

The room was vast and magnificent. Huge, thick bearskin rugs were stretched upon the floor. Stuffed animals and birds were displayed in glass cases and on shelves. An enormous elk's head, with branching antlers, hung above a mammoth mantelpiece. Horned heads, reptiles, giant game fish, and gaudy specimens of tropical butterflies with brilliant, jewelled wings covered the walls. An exhibit of small birds mounted in lifelike poses occupied a glass cabinet in a corner. Rare weapons of all kinds hung on walls and racks.

"What a valuable collection!" cried Ronald in awe.

"Yes, this room must be worth a fortune in itself!" affirmed Kay, gazing around in deep interest. "We must tell Tom Curran about it so that he can be on the alert to protect it too."

She ran upstairs, calling the watchman's name. He answered from the big dining hall. As Kay entered the room, she was just in time to see him pry loose one of the stones on the hearth of the fireplace with an iron crowbar.

"What are you doing?" she asked eagerly.

Curran replied, "I felt one of these slabs move when I walked here. I wanted to find out why."

"We can look at it in a minute," said Kay, "but first come and see what we've found in the basement!"

Curran dropped his crowbar and followed her. He left the heavy oblong rock loosened, but in place.

No sooner had the footsteps of himself and the girl died away than there came the sound of stealthy footsteps. There was a click and the squeaking of hinges. A draft of cool air signified that someone had opened an outside door.

A dark figure in a black mask slipped like a shadow into the dining hall. At sight of the crowbar on the hearth, the man stopped, then advanced noiselessly. A jerk on the tool soon lifted out the stone.

With a quick glance over one shoulder, the intruder stooped to the hole underneath. Hastily he pulled out a stout wooden chest. Before he could pause long enough to replace the cover, voices and steps sounded from the stairway. The sneak thief leaped from the mansion on shoes that were muffled in felt, as softly and nimbly as a mouse. With the chest in his arms, he vanished!

"Look, look!" cried Kay, entering the room. "Someone has pried up the stone."

She raced to the open door and caught a glimpse of a fleeing figure. By the way he was running, with a box under his arm, Kay had no doubt but that he had found something valuable. The girl also caught sight of Martin Mulligan, bent over a flower bed, industriously weeding. She shouted to him:

"Martin! Martin! Quick! Catch that thief!"

XVIII

The Seventh Step

Martin Mulligan, on his knees pulling weeds, had not seen the sneak thief, and the man had not noticed him. At Kay's cry of alarm, the handyman stood up and looked around, confused.

"There he goes!" the girl shouted, pointing.

Mulligan caught a brief glimpse of a man running, and he tried to chase him. Unfortunately the sailor was heavy, and his seagoing gait did not carry him very fast on shore.

The robber, on the other hand, fled like the shadow of a bird. The diminishing sound of feet padding down the lane faded away. The masked intruder had escaped again!

Puffing and panting, the seaman was forced to give up the pursuit and return to the house. He found the others excitedly wondering what had been hidden under the hearth.

"To think that landlubber snatched it right from under my nose!" raved Martin Mulligan furiously.

Kay decided to go outside and do some measuring of the newly made footprints of the intruder. As she and Ronald looked at them, they were astounded at the kind of marks they found.

"That man had something over the soles of his

shoes!" exclaimed the girl. "He was taking no chances of being checked up by his footprints."

At this moment the young people heard a shout from a pasture back of the stables. This place had been fixed up as a riding ring. Cantering around was Chris Eaton in the midst of her first lesson. Kay and Ronald hurried over and stood outside the fence, inside of which the gaily garbed pupil was making a spectacle of herself.

Cody, who was still stiff and a trifle weak, was being assisted by Jimmy. The stableman looked disgusted when Chris uttered affected little shrieks of pretended fear in order to get the cowboy to hold her in the saddle.

When she realized that she could please him best by learning quickly, the girl tried to follow his instructions about trotting around the enclosure. She gave little delighted cries of triumph as she bounded up and down in the saddle.

"That gal bounces so high you could take that ten-gallon hat of hers and throw it clean under her without hitting either her or the saddle!" commented Jimmy sourly to Ronald.

"Do you think she'll ever learn to ride?" Kay heard Cody say to Jimmy.

"Well," drawled the bow-legged stableman, "so far she and the horse don't seem to get together very often!"

Chris herself was highly satisfied with her performance. "Please get my camera, Jimmy!" she wheedled. "It's over there on that fence post. I want you to take a good picture of me to show at school."

"I ain't much of a picture-taker!" the little man protested, but he did as she asked him to.

Chris tried various poses, calling out, "How do I look? Wait, is that better? How's this?"

"You need more action!" said the groom in disgust, and barked harshly at the horse, "Giddap!"

Chris, taken off her guard, nearly catapulted over the mount's head. She saved herself by lying flat on her chest and throwing both arms wildly around the neck of the horse. Her feet flew out of the stirrups, and her hat dropped. At that instant Jimmy snapped a picture of her!

"That'll be a great picture for the bulletin board of Carmont High," grinned Ronald as he and Kay returned to the house.

Chris was the first of a number of riders who soon made Cody's Riding Club popular. It became Brantwood's biggest attraction and drew members from towns as far away as Dunbar City.

"The trouble with all this success is that now Cody will insist upon purchasing the property," said Bill one day with a worried frown.

"Yes," responded Kay, "and we are nowhere near solving the mansion's secrets!"

"And I can't get any word of Peter Greely," complained the lawyer.

"At least there is one good thing," reflected Kay. "Having so many people coming and going on the place appears to have scared away our masked man! He doesn't seem to have been here lately."

Kay had told her cousin about the appearance of the mysterious woman whom the twins had seen at the Brantwood station. Now she asked him what he thought of the idea of her going to Dunbar City to try to locate this person.

"Go by all means," he urged. "She may be a link in this chain of puzzles."

As it turned out, the trip was not necessary. The very next morning at the depot the twins nudged Kay excitedly.

"There she is!" they hissed in Kay's ear.

"Who?" asked their friend in bewilderment.

"The woman we told you about! The one who was poking at the staircase in the Greely mansion!"

Kay looked carefully at the woman who stood on the platform. Yes, it was certainly the same person! Kay recognized her dumpy little figure, her plain coat and demure black hat. She even carried the same worn shopping bag!

The train was now thundering into the station. Kay managed to follow the woman closely and get a seat next to her in the coach. The girl smiled pleasantly. The other traveller smiled back. She was a friendly, chatty person, and soon was talking about her recent visit to relatives in town.

"I'm going back home to New York now," she confided to Kay. "You see, I'm a trained nurse and I have to get back to work after my little holiday with the Cookes. I must keep employed to support myself."

"It must be hard work," said the schoolgirl, trying to lead the conversation around to the Greely house.

"Yes, some cases are not easy. I had one in Brantwood some time ago. An old man. He died."

"I live in Brantwood," said Kay. "I wonder if he was anyone I knew?"

"He was an invalid by the name of Greely, Manuel Greely."

Kay could hardly suppress her excitement. Here was a real clue!

"Yes, I've heard of him," Kay replied cautiously. "It's rumored he was very wealthy, and had a fortune hidden in his house."

"He was very eccentric," replied the nurse. "He used to speak about hiding money around the place. I laughed about it and told my relatives how he talked. I guess they started the rumor that the mansion was a sort of gold mine!" she said goodhumoredly.

Kay encouraged the woman to continue her story.

"Old Mr. Greely would say to me, 'Miss Cooke'—my name's Sara Cooke—'if people knew about my wealth they'd try to rob me. They're always trying to rob me as it is. I have to guard against that all the time.'"

Miss Cooke laughed.

"That's the way he would worry about his possessions. I'd try to calm his fears, but he would sit up in bed and say, 'I'll fool the robbers! I've got my fortune hidden away where nobody can find it!' You see, he was sick and feverish and I had to humor him. I thought his mind was wandering."

"You mean he didn't know what he was saying?" asked Kay, afraid the train would reach Carmont before she could secure enough information.

"I thought he was delirious a good deal of the time," the nurse answered. "And I guess he was! He told me a dozen times that if I didn't get my full salary I was to look inside a certain step in the staircase. Of course, I thought he was just babbling crazily. I didn't take what he said seriously."

"Did you ever look in the step?" asked Kay quickly.

A glance out of the car window showed that they were approaching Carmont. Kay hoped she would get an answer before she would have to leave the train.

"Yes," replied the nurse, "I did look in the step once! After the old man passed away, part of my salary was unpaid. Mr. Greely died without a will and nothing was found with which to pay his bills. So—"

"Yes?" prompted Kay eagerly.

The train was stopping!

"So on the spur of the moment I went out to the estate to see if there was anything to what Mr. Greely had told me. I suppose I should have taken a policeman with me. I later did send the key I had to the mansion to headquarters."

"All out for Carmont!" shouted the conductor.

High school students and others piled out of the train. Betty and Wendy left slowly, eyeing Kay and the stranger curiously.

"So you looked—" urged Kay in an agony of suspense.

"A-l-l a-b-o-a-r-d!" the voice chanted again. "Next stop Dun-bar City!"

Outside the train the twins were jumping up and down in a panic that Kay might be carried to the next station. The locomotive whistled loudly. Trainmen signalled to the engineer to start.

"Oh, please wait a second!" Wendy pleaded. "Someone else is getting off!"

"So you looked," Kay prodded, already standing in the car aisle. "What did you find?"

XIX

The Figure in Hiding

"You'd better get off, dearie," warned Sara Cooke. "Didn't you say this was your station?"

"Oh, but I can't leave until I hear the end of your story!" protested Kay. "What did you find?"

"Nothing!" said the nurse calmly. "The step was empty! So I didn't have a thing to report to the authorities."

Kay groaned aloud. "Good-bye!" she cried, and rushed off the train to leap into the arms of the anxious and disapproving twins.

"Tell us," Wendy said eagerly. "What did she find in the step?"

"Nothing at all!" replied Kay.

"That's what she told *you*," commented Betty suspiciously. "But she may have found a thousand dollars!"

"We'll have to get in touch with her again," Kay decided. "She's a relative of the Cookes in Brantwood and seems to be a very nice person."

Kay's mind kept returning to her friend's distrustful idea about the nurse; yet she could not believe that the woman was dishonest. It was not until her chemistry class that she suddenly was jolted from all thought of Sara Cooke.

"Today we'll have a quiz on the subject of

perfume," Doctor Staunton announced unexpectedly to his students. "Get your papers and pencils ready, please. I will write the questions on the blackboard."

Poor Kay! Many eyes in the room were turned on her, and Chris Eaton's face wore a malicious smirk of satisfaction. The embarrassed girl found it hard to keep her mind on the technical side of the subject. All she could think of was the loss she had caused the perfume factory in Dunbar City.

"I wonder if I'll ever be able to locate any ambergris and repay the management for what I did," she reflected miserably.

In her pocketbook at that very moment was a letter in reply to one from her to a company owning a fishing fleet. The answer was discouraging. All the girl's search in the newspapers and magazines had failed to help her. Vaguely she wondered to whom old Mr. Greely had sold his supply of the scarce and valuable substance.

After class the twins rushed up to Kay. "I could hit Chris for the way she looked at you," stormed Betty. "It wouldn't surprise me if she made you have that accident at the Boswell plant and she's letting you take all the blame."

"Let's go horseback riding this afternoon and forget the whole thing," suggested Wendy.

Kay agreed, and the girls set out for the Greely estate about half past three. Reaching the stables, they found Chris Eaton issuing orders to poor Jimmy.

"She acts as if she owns the place!" grumbled Betty.

Chris certainly had an overbearing air of ownership. She paused to supervise the stableman's saddling of some mares. Without paying any attention to her, he helped Wendy to mount a quiet, gentle horse called Ladybird.

"She can't have that one today!" Chris objected. "Mr. Cody promised Ladybird to me for this afternoon!"

"I have Pinto saddled for you," said Jimmy firmly.

"I don't want Pinto!" Chris pouted. "He nearly threw me the day you took my picture. I'd rather ride Wyoming."

"I have an English saddle on Wyoming for this young lady," said Jimmy, helping Betty into the stirrup. "You want a Western one, don't you?" he asked.

Kay, who had often ridden with Bill and was used to the sport, now mounted a lively horse called Black Hawk. She signalled to the girls to follow her, leaving Chris to indulge her bad temper as much as she liked.

"Mr. Cody has developed some very pretty pathways through these woods," said Kay admiringly.

The horses as well as the girls seemed to enjoy jogging along under arching trees and past sweet-smelling shrubs.

"It's lovely here," said Betty.

"A good place to chase the cobwebs from one's brain," added Wendy.

"What's that ahead?" asked Betty suddenly. "Not a wild animal, I hope!"

She drew her horse to a slow walk. Kay urged hers forward to see what lay on the ground before them.

"It's just a dog," she called back. "A big one gnawing a bone—oh, it's that same police dog."

"The one that kept us in the closet?" cried Wendy.

She was trying vainly to hold her mount to a standstill as she timidly eyed the animal.

"Ride past him quietly and maybe he won't take his mind off the bone," said Kay.

She followed her own advice and started forward. The dog raised its head and growled in an ugly way, showing great white teeth. The girls urged their mounts on. As they passed the smaller animal, it snarled savagely, leaped to its feet, and sprang at the nose of Kay's horse.

Black Hawk sidestepped in terror, rose on his hind legs, then bolted down the trail. The dog then whirled on Betty's Wyoming, barking at his heels and sending him off on a fast gallop. Wendy's gentle Ladybird, also frightened, turned and ran off on a different bridle path from the one the others were following.

As Kay pounded away in a wild cross-country run, she heard a sharp, insistent whistle. The dog heard it too. Instantly the well-trained animal stopped barking and streaked in the direction of the piercing note.

Kay managed to control her frightened horse long enough to catch a fleeting glimpse of a man standing well back from the path. The dog raced toward him and both disappeared into the woods.

"The masked stranger without his mask!" Kay gasped. "And I can't possibly go after him."

Betty came galloping up, branches of the trees slashing at her face, her stirrups flying. Kay succeeded in stopping her friend's horse. Wendy also approached with Ladybird well under control.

"What are you looking at?" she asked as she saw Kay gazing intently into the forest.

"I saw the owner of the police dog over there," her friend replied. "I got a look at him. I'm sure he's Lamont, the model in the Eatmor advertisement. I'm so angry he got away again!"

"I'd rather not meet him in these woods," quavered Wendy. "Let's turn back before the sun sets."

When the friends reached the mansion, Kay hurried to tell Tom Curran about the person with the dog. He immediately set out to scout along the trails in the hope of locating the prowler.

"Let's stay around the house awhile," suggested

Kay. "Maybe Tom will bring some news. In the meantime we can do a little exploring here."

"Oh!" Wendy said suddenly. "I just remembered that there was a red 'X' on that built-in bookcase in the second-floor library!"

"Good!" cried Kay.

Three pairs of russet riding boots instantly clattered upstairs, hot on a new trail!

"Here are the bookshelves," said Betty, as the girls reached the spot. "But which one conceals the treasure?"

"It will be a chore to find out," sighed Wendy. "The shelves reach almost to the ceiling!"

"I'm going to climb up and examine every one," declared Kay energetically.

"Here are some empty wooden boxes we can pile up as a sort of ladder," suggested Betty.

These were put one on top of another. As the twins tried to steady the uncertain steps, the Tracey girl went up.

"Do you see anything?" Wendy asked, watching Kay's precarious perch anxiously.

"A lot of dust!" answered the climber, sneezing.

"If that's all, you better come down before you fall down," advised Betty.

"Wait a minute!" cried Kay, her voice rising sharply with excitement. "There's something behind this top shelf."

As she spoke, Curran returned from his futile hunt, uneasy about leaving the house unguarded. He entered the kitchen, hoping nothing had happened in his absence. At that very moment a deafening crash roared through the house.

The watchman leaped upstairs, three steps at a time. He was directed to the scene of the noise by more clatter and an outburst of shrill, girlish voices. Tom looked into the old library and saw the three girls, one of them on the floor amid a pile of boxes! Laughing in relief to find no one was hurt, he withdrew.

"I'm going to climb up there again!" said Kay with determination. "I was just about to say when I fell that I had found a secret wall safe!"

XX

Perfume Puzzle

Once again Kay climbed on top of the piled boxes to examine the wall space back of the highest shelf.

"There's a sort of nook or compartment here," she announced. "It would have been hidden by books if they hadn't been removed."

"Anything in it?" asked Betty.

"No. Oh, yes! I just touched a spring and a panel has slid back!" Kay cried excitedly.

"What's behind it?" asked the twins in chorus.

"A safe!" answered Kay, teetering perilously. "It has a metal door, and it's latched but not locked."

Although Betty and Wendy were extremely eager to climb up themselves, they remained below, firmly holding the pile of crates.

"Find anything?" they asked presently.

"A lot of jars," came the reply.

"Bring down a couple of them and let's see what's inside!"

Clutching them tightly in her arms, Kay began a careful descent. This time she landed safely with her load.

"Quick, quick! Open them!" begged Betty.

"I wonder whether the jars hold sparkling jewels or gleaming gold?" Wendy murmured romantically.

"They're not heavy enough for gold," observed

Kay, unscrewing the lid of one of the light metal containers as fast as she could.

Betty and Wendy peered over her shoulder, impatient for a sight of the contents. An exclamation of disappointment escaped them.

"What peculiar stuff!" cried Betty. "What is it?"

"Some kind of wax," Wendy suggested.

"It looks as if it ought to have a horrible odor!" Betty declared, wrinkling up her nose.

Kay gave an investigating sniff. "It's all right!" she said. "It has a faint, clean, earthy smell; that's all."

"What can it be?" wondered Wendy. "Is it valuable, do you suppose?"

"It's beeswax!" cried Betty decidedly.

"Oh, no, it couldn't be!" Kay disagreed.

"What, then?"

"I'm not sure," Kay answered slowly.

She had a suspicion in her own mind but hesitated about saying it. Could it be the substance Martin Mulligan said he and old Mr. Greely had scooped up on the ocean? If so, was it what the perfume factory had used? The valuable stuff she had spilled?

"Ambergris!" she said aloud. "Oh, if it turns out to be, maybe I could buy it from the estate and give it to the Boswell plant!"

"You said there were a lot of boxes. If they all contain ambergris, they must be worth a lot of money," exclaimed Betty.

"Of course we can't be sure yet," said Kay, "but Martin said he and Mr. Greely had found something they thought was ambergris."

"Let's hurry home with these jars and ask your cousin," urged Betty.

"I'm afraid to carry anything so valuable with us. That man with the dog might hold us up and steal it," advised Wendy.

"I think Wendy is right," agreed Kay. "I vote we hide it where we found it and give Bill the responsibility of taking it to town!"

"Second the motion!" said Betty heartily.

The two containers of mysterious wax were restored to their original hiding place and the discoverers started home with the news. On their way out they passed Mulligan, who was mowing the lawn.

"Now ain't this a fine pastime for a sailor?" he asked bitterly. "I'm getting homesick for the sea!"

"When Bill pays you, you'll be able to buy a train ticket and go back to your boat," Kay encouraged the man.

Martin Mulligan looked discontented. "My wages aren't very big," he said. "I only wish I had the money Mr. Greely owed me if he sold that ambergris! After all, I got it in my fishing boat. He took it to find out the value. Too bad he died without letting me know about it!"

Kay signalled to the twins, with a twitch of her eyebrows, not to say anything. "We mustn't raise his hopes," she explained later. "Even if the stuff is ambergris, I'm not sure the court would allow Mulligan to benefit from the sale of it."

"I really don't understand about the waxy substance," confessed Betty in a puzzled way.

"They told us it came from a sick whale," Kay reminded her.

"I've made up a poem about it," said Wendy, looking distantly from a window in the car.

"Beneath the sea, mysterious and deep,
Strange creatures live and their secrets keep.

The oyster's wounds make pearls within its shell.
The great whale, suffering, leaves a gift as well

*To preserve scents of flowers touched by sun.
Pray tell us, creatures queer, how this is done,*

*So that, from you, this secret we shall know:
How, out of pain, we may make beauty grow!"*

"Why, Wendy Worth! I think that's perfectly beautiful!" Betty cried. "It's the best poem you ever composed."

Wendy flushed with pride. Kay added her congratulations.

As the girls drove down Hemlock Lane, they met Clarence Cody, coming up to the mansion. He rode one horse and was leading another.

"I found my Brownie!" he announced happily, as Kay stopped the car to greet him.

"Great!" she cried. "Where was he?"

"Abandoned in the far pasture. Apparently someone had taken him to ride, because he was saddled and bridled. When I found him, he was being chased by a police dog that was snapping at his heels."

"Poor Brownie!" Wendy sympathized.

"That dog is almost ruining my business!" complained Cody gloomily. "It runs out of the woods and jumps at horses and riders. I'm afraid it may cause a serious accident some day! I think I'll lasso the beast and tie it up."

"That's a good idea. I think you'll find that his master is the one who stole your horse," said Kay, as she started away.

Reaching home, she told the latest developments of the mystery to Bill. He was amazed to hear about the ambergris and praised his cousin and her friends for their cleverness.

"Suppose we all drive out there after dinner," he suggested, turning to Kay's mother.

This was agreed upon. During the meal the entire subject of conversation was the Greely affair.

"We'll never know the full extent of the man's wealth," said Bill, "unless we catch the masked intruder and get back the plans. The police have not been able to locate him, although they are watching the property and have tried to follow the clue you found to his whereabouts, Kay."

"Yes, if he is in the town of Brantwood, he ought to be easy to capture," remarked Mrs. Tracey.

"I certainly wish I could get in touch with Peter Greely," sighed Bill.

"That pilot owes you and Kay far more than he knows!" said Mrs. Tracey.

"He owes me some new clothes!" laughed Kay, showing a three-cornered tear in her best school skirt. "Every time I go out to the mansion exploring, I rip something or else get very dirty!"

"Never mind, I'll mend and clean them," replied her mother. "It's all in a good cause! I only hope that you don't get hurt in any of these escapades!"

"Don't worry, I won't!" Kay assured her.

A few minutes later Bill drove Kay and her mother to the mansion to bring back the mysterious wax before the masked man had a chance to steal it. The attorney was as puzzled by the material as the girls had been.

"This will have to be examined by experts to determine whether it is true ambergris or not," he said. "Kay, you and I will drive to the Boswell Perfume Company in Dunbar City and have them look at it. If it is genuine, perhaps they will pay a good price for it!"

"If it really is ambergris, I wish I could buy some of it from the estate to give to them," remarked Kay wistfully. "I feel awful about spilling the stuff."

"I'm sure that can be arranged," the lawyer said.

On the following Saturday morning, she accompanied her cousin to Dunbar City. Both the manager, Mr. Lubin, and the president, Mr. Boswell, were deeply interested in seeing what the callers had brought.

An examination of the material was begun to prove whether or not it was ambergris. Bill was closeted with the officers of the company for some time, discussing this analysis and talking business.

Kay, meanwhile, wandered through the sweet-scented factory, examining and admiring the manufacturing processes. Suddenly her eyes fell upon an advertisement for one of their perfumes. Thumbtacked to the wall was a colored poster showing a handsome man in evening clothes. He was bending over a beautiful lady who wore gardenias.

The picture so startled Kay that she stood stock still and gasped. The model in the poster was none other than Lester Lamont, the person she suspected of being the masked man!

Since Bill was still in conference with the perfume makers, Kay went alone to inquire at the outer office for information about the figure in the picture.

"I will refer you to our Mr. Washburn," replied the clerk.

Kay was ushered into the private office of the company's advertising manager. She explained that her lawyer cousin was trying to get in touch with a man who looked like the model.

"He's Lester Lamont," answered the manager, "and I'm sure we have his address. We keep in touch with him because we often use him in our publicity illustrations."

While a file clerk was looking up the model's address, Mr. Washburn indicated other posters on the wall, in which the same handsome man was featured.

Kay sat looking at them, puzzling about this good-looking person. He certainly did not look like a housebreaker and a thief.

She had come to no conclusion in her thoughts, when the smiling file clerk bustled in and handed a brown envelope to the manager. Mr. Washburn pulled out some typewritten sheets and scanned them for a moment.

Kay now had high hopes of finding Lester Lamont and perhaps putting an end to the thievery at Greely Mansion.

XXI

Sad News

As Kay waited for the advertising man to give her the information, her mind worked far ahead. She would catch the thief, she would recover the stolen plans, and she would check all the hiding places marked with the red "X's."

"Here is the address you want, Miss Tracey," said Mr. Washburn finally. "We have Lamont listed as staying at the Dunbar City Hotel."

All Kay's hopes crashed! She managed to reply, "We traced him there, but he had left. We heard that he had gone from Dunbar City to Brantwood. I was hoping you knew where he moved to."

"I'm afraid not," answered the manager. "I can only say, that when he next reports for an assignment, we will get his present address and notify you."

With this slim hope the girl had to be satisfied. "We are no nearer finding him than we were before!" she thought sadly.

Kay was in a gloomy mood when finally Bill joined her. Her cousin, on the other hand, was in high spirits.

"Good news!" he cried. "You found real ambergris! This company is willing to pay a good price for it!"

Kay was very excited over this good luck, and could hardly wait to tell the twins. Needless to say, they were delighted over the development.

This happy frame of mind kept the trio in a good mood over the weekend, and they wondered what new surprises the old mansion might reveal.

Kay met the twins at the station in time for the school train. She hurried to the railroad platform, humming happily to herself.

Betty and Wendy did not notice her approach. Betty's blonde head and Wendy's dark one were bent over a newspaper which the former held. They were so absorbed that Kay's sudden greeting made them jump.

"Have you seen it?" they asked.

"Seen what?" Kay questioned.

Unable to speak, Betty silently handed the newspaper to her friend, while Wendy pointed to an article on the front page. Kay tucked her school books under one arm and grappled with the newspaper. On the front page of the Carmont Daily News a headline read:

PILOT
CRASHES IN ENGLAND

Government Flier
Reported Dead

Peter Greely, heir to the estate of the late Manuel Greely of Brantwood, is said to have been pilot of a plane which crashed yesterday somewhere in England.

The young airplane pilot is thought to have flown a plane of special design on a secret European mission for the U.S. Government.

Details of the accident are not yet known but it is reported that young Greely was killed.

Stunned by this news, Kay and the twins could find nothing to say to one another. Wendy's eyes were wet.

Just then the train came roaring into Brantwood station. The three friends climbed aboard silently. The numbness which followed their shock at the bad news did not wear off until the train pulled in at Carmont.

"It's awfully sad," said Wendy tremulously. "He was so good-looking and so nice!"

"Now he'll never need the fortune we've found," sighed Betty with a sniffle.

"We have those lovely prints he gave us as keepsakes," Kay reminded the others. Then she added, "This will complicate things for Bill. It will be a problem to settle everything, because there was no will and there isn't any other relative to inherit the estate!"

It was no wonder that the three girls were inattentive and preoccupied during all their classes. They could not keep their minds on work and did so poorly in their lessons that Doctor Staunton gave each of them a sharp reprimand in chemistry class. Chris Eaton could not repress a sly smile of satisfaction to hear a scolding given to students whose school work usually was far better than her own.

"Teacher's pets certainly got theirs this morning," she giggled maliciously to Ronald Earle in study period.

Ronald, who had heard the sad news, was as gloomy as Kay. He glared at Chris and walked off to a seat as far as possible from her.

"We might go for a horseback ride this afternoon to cheer ourselves up," Kay suggested. "I don't feel like having a thing to do with exploring the mansion for its secrets," she said listlessly. "I've lost all heart for the search."

"So have I," admitted Betty sadly.

"I think a horseback ride is a great idea," said Wendy. "It will do us all good."

As this opinion was unanimous, the downhearted friends changed into riding clothes after school and went out to Cody's Club. Wendy greeted her former saddle horse, Ladybird, with real affection. There seemed to be a certain feeling and understanding between Wendy and this gentle horse.

But Betty, on the dashing Wyoming, and Kay, on the sprightly Black Hawk, did not do so well, even under Jimmy's instruction. Their fiery mounts could not understand the mood of their sober riders.

"Oh, forget it," sighed Betty. "I'm bouncing worse than Chris Eaton! There's no use. I'm just not in the mood for this today. I'm going to quit!"

To Jimmy's consternation Kay said, "I will, too!"

Dismounting, the twins and Kay strolled automatically toward Greely mansion. They met Tom Curran, who had come out of the house for a moment to speak to Martin Mulligan. The handyman was working in the front yard.

"Are you going to tell them about poor Peter, Kay?" asked Betty.

"Oh, yes," replied her friend. "I think they should know about it."

The news report of the Greely heir was met solemnly by both men. As Mulligan had never seen Peter, naturally he was not as impressed as the others. Tom looked quite dismal.

"It kind of makes me lose heart about keeping watch over the old place," he said.

At that moment someone sneaked to the rear of the house. While Kay and the twins stood talking with the two men on the front lawn, this figure slipped into the mansion through a secret entrance. The stealthy prowler, of course, was a very handsome, athletic young man who kept his face completely covered with a black silk mask!

He went quickly into the basement and boldly advanced into the underground passage with the directness of a person who knows exactly what he is doing! Having covered the damp and musty distance of the hidden corridor, he now forced open the door at the end of the hall with a set of pocket tools, and strode into the trophy room.

The masked man was equipped with an excellent flashlight. He swung it about, wasting no time, and found the electric switch. This he hurriedly snapped on and went to work without gazing at the wonders of the remarkable room. He was there to get something and get it in a hurry!

Pausing for the space of a breath, he listened for footsteps. There was not a sound. Feeling safe for the moment, he walked straight to the wall on which hung the head of a mammoth polar bear! It was a splendid specimen and was preserved in a savagely lifelike manner. Its huge mouth was open wide. Snow-white teeth showed viciously against the blood red of the painted gums and tongue.

As the man's weight dragged on the jaw, the animal's entire head, which was hinged, bent forward. Revealed was a small safe, embedded inside the back of the neck, which was mounted on a polished wooden plaque.

The nimble fingers opened the safe and dislodged its contents. Into one palm fell a handful of large, rough lumps of metal of a dirty yellow color. For a minute the man paused to examine these objects. He felt them with thumb and fingers, appraised their weight by lifting the handful up and down.

Another sharp glance at his discovery seemed to satisfy him. They were nuggets of pure gold as large as hazelnuts! A sly smile was hidden behind the silken mask, as this treasure was slipped hastily into a worn leather pouch and stuffed deep into the robber's pocket.

The bear's head was pushed back into place. No one could have told that it ever had been touched!

Now the sneak thief rapidly reversed his procedure. He snapped off the light, and took one final farewell glance at the polar bear. It seemed to snarl mutely in the flashlight's yellow stream. This long gleam swung away and pointed into the doorway. It pierced the darkness of the underground passage.

With a low laugh, the cat-footed prowler ran quickly down the corridor toward the secret place where he had entered. He moved with the soft-footed silence and lithe grace once a part of those wild animals whose heads hung stiff and still in the trophy room.

Overhead came the thump of feet. The marauder halted. He listened, crept forward cautiously, then hurried quickly through a door.

He leaped too hastily. It was not the exit he thought it was. With a terrific splash he fell headlong into a deep, dark pool of icy water! Down, down, he sank, the violence of his fall sending him deeper and still deeper! The water closed over his head.

The masked intruder had made his first mistake. He had stepped through the wrong door!

XXII

The Green Ghost

Sputtering, the surprised robber came to the surface of the water. The silk mask had been splashed off and now floated, limp and bedraggled, in the pool, like a black lily pad. There were, in fact, green lily pads with ghostly white blossoms dotting the surface. Various other plants grew thickly over the water. Their snaky roots and wet, clammy leaves entangled the frantic swimmer.

The man had fallen into Manuel Greely's indoor marine garden. Neglected and uncared for, its plants had grown wild, filling the pond until it was as thick as a jungle! The swimmer now thrashed about, startling frogs and goldfish from their peace by his sudden and unwelcome invasion of their slimy realm.

Meanwhile, Tom Curran and Mulligan had gone to the village for much-needed supplies. Kay Tracey and the Worths had been left temporarily in charge of the grim mansion.

"We haven't seen the trophy room that you and Ronald discovered," said Betty. "Please show it to us, Kay."

"All right," her friend agreed gladly.

"I don't like underground passages," observed Wendy as they started.

Nevertheless she followed the others. Soon they were standing in the dark room. Kay dramatically snapped on the light and instantly all the beasts and birds flashed into view.

"For goodness sake!" gasped Betty, her mouth wide open in amazement.

"What's that sound?" asked Wendy, looking around nervously.

"What does it sound like?" asked Kay.

"I thought it was a cough," said Wendy, and she added apologetically, "but maybe not. Since my trapdoor scare, I'm always thinking I hear coughs."

"Well, it can't be this big polar bear barking," remarked Betty jokingly, "because it's stuffed!"

"It did sound like a bark; a kind of muffled bark," declared Wendy with conviction. "Oh, I hear splashing water!"

The three girls listened intently.

"I hear something, too," Kay admitted.

Wendy looked worriedly at all the heads and horns, birds and beasts that stared from the walls.

"Let's get out of here!" she cried.

Without delay the twins did so. Down the lighted passage they stampeded when a hideous figure appeared suddenly in a doorway.

This weird apparition, dripping wet, swayed uncertainly before them. It was horribly draped in a slimy green veil. Streamers of dripping vines hung over his head and hair. Its uplifted arms trailed wet and drooping festoons of stuff like seaweed. The twins shrieked and ran madly toward the stairway.

Kay was left to face the awful creature alone! In spite of her bravery Kay was frightened. She watched as though hypnotized. Silently waving its arms, the green ghost snapped out the light and seemed to float away. As this eerie figure vanished, Kay's courage returned.

"That was nothing more nor less than the same masked figure in a new disguise," she told herself. Kay stumbled up the dark cellar stairs, berating herself that she had not tried to capture him. "I wonder how he got soaked," she mused.

When Kay reached the kitchen, the twins grabbed her in relief. "Oh, you—you're safe!" they gasped. "We thought you were right behind us but then you didn't come. Where did the ghost go?"

"Pull yourselves together," urged Kay calmly. "I'm sure that was our same housebreaker in a new outfit."

"This mansion must have all sorts of secret entrances and exits," spoke up Betty, not knowing she had hit upon the truth.

"Until the men come back, I think we ought to stay outdoors," Wendy quavered. "I don't want to be in this place with that—that thief," she added, going to the door.

As the girls stepped into the garden, they heard a door slam. In a moment a lithe figure, that did not look like a ghost, but like a Halloween masquerader ran across an open space and disappeared into the woods. Kay would have chased him, but her friends held back.

"Well, maybe you're right," she agreed. "While that man's not around, though, let's do some more treasure hunting. I'm determined to search the sun-room. There was a red 'X' marked in that spot, I seem to remember."

The spot to which Kay led the twins was a bright, cheerful place full of wide windows, through which the comforting sunshine was streaming.

"This is better than the cellar," approved Betty.

"What lovely wood carving!" Wendy said.

"Yes, isn't it?" agreed Kay. "Tom Curran says this was called the flower room because it was kept full of plants, and besides, you see the carvings are all floral decorations."

The girls examined and exclaimed over the exquisite designs on the wall panels.

"Look at this little wooden bee perched on a blossom!" Betty cried in delight. "It looks almost alive!"

"So does this tiny humming bird sipping from some honeysuckle!" Wendy called. "You can almost see the spray move."

"I wouldn't know where to begin hunting treasure," sighed Betty. She began experimentally pressing, pulling and trying to unscrew the bird, the bee, and some buds and blossoms. "None of these opens," she reported.

"I'll try this little Cupid," said Kay.

The central figure in the carved design was that of a dancing Cupid. This chubby little god poised gaily on tiptoe amid graceful garlands and nosegays. The girls could not help smiling at him!

Kay gently ran her fingers over his small form. This appealed to the fancy of Wendy, who murmured dreamily:

> *"Little Love, tell us, pray,*
> *Where is Treasure tucked away?*
> *Do these flowers hold just honey,*
> *Or do they conceal some money?"*

"It can't be true!" Kay squealed excitedly. "Look! A treasure chest!"

The Cupid had swung around obligingly as if Wendy had spoken some magic charm to make him tell his secret! There now was exposed a little niche that had been hidden behind his back.

A very small, beautiful, hand-carved chest lay in this nook. Kay lifted it out. Carefully raising the ornate lid, she found within a closely fitting box. Inside this second container was something neatly wrapped in tissue paper.

XXIII

Kay's Dream

―――――――◆―――――――

"Hide it quickly, Kay!" warned Betty. "I hear footsteps!"

The girl prudently slipped the contents of the nook into her pocket.

"It's only Tom Curran and Martin Mulligan," said Wendy in relief.

"Who did you think it was?" asked Curran, laughing at the girls' concern.

"I was afraid it might be the green ghost again," shuddered Wendy.

"The what?" asked Tom in surprise, while Mulligan burst into a loud ha-ha at the title.

Kay quickly explained about their recent adventure in the trophy room. While Mulligan and Tom strode off to investigate the basement, Kay pushed the little Cupid back into position. With her find still in her pocket she led the way outside to her car.

"It's getting late. We must go home," Kay suggested. "Suppose you two stay at my house for supper," she urged the twins. "We'll show the treasure chest to Bill and find out what's in it!"

After stopping at the Worths' home to let their mother know that they would be at Kay's, the friends hurried on.

"Bill's here already. I see him through the window!" Kay cried eagerly, jumping from the car.

Betty and Wendy ran after her and the three companions burst into the living room. Kay's mother greeted them with a smile.

"On time for supper for once," she laughed.

"Yes, and see what we brought with us!" exclaimed Kay, pulling the little chest from her pocket and laying it on the table.

"More Greely treasure?" Mrs. Tracey queried.

"We found it at the mansion but we haven't looked at it yet!" said Kay, unwrapping the tissue paper with hands that trembled with excitement.

Bill joined the group that clustered around, eyeing the package curiously. As the last wrapping fell away, out rolled a generous handful of lovely unset jewels! A little chorus of ohs and ahs went up. The girls gave soft cries of delight as the lamplight brought out the fierce reds, golden glows, and glittering sparks in the gems.

Forgetting everything but the beauty before them, the three friends revelled in the changing colors. Mrs. Tracey, however, had the presence of mind to draw down the window shades. This time no spying eyes observed the pile of jewels glistening in the light on the library table!

After a few minutes more of admiration, the family and friends sat down at the dining room table. Supper was eaten in the best of spirits.

The evening slipped by so quickly that everyone was surprised when they noticed that it was late.

"I'll drive the Worths home," Bill offered smilingly. "Come along, Kay. We'll stop for sodas."

The twins and the Traceys went to a popular drugstore. Soon they were seated together cheerfully sucking sodas through straws, or spooning up ice cream. Around them was the stir of people coming and going. Suddenly Chris Eaton entered with a noisy group of her friends, both boys and girls. Chattering loudly about some snapshots she wanted to show the crowd, the girl asked at the counter for a film she had left to be developed.

"Wait till you see me riding in true cowgirl style!" Chris bragged. "The horse was bucking his hardest but he couldn't throw me!" she boasted.

"Here you are," said the clerk, handing Chris a brown envelope.

Her friends crowded close to see the photographs. Chris displayed them unsuspectingly. As they passed around the snapshots Jimmy had taken, snickers broke out.

"Look at this one! Ha-ha!"

"Let me see!"

The snapshots were excellent and cruelly clear. They showed the proud cowgirl half falling off her horse and obviously scared stiff! Beet-red, Chris retreated from the store in embarrassed confusion.

"Poor Chris!" laughed Kay. "I wonder if she'll ever show up again at the riding school."

"Let's go out tomorrow and see," giggled Betty.

Apparently the Eaton girl's embarrassment did not last long, for she reached the Greely estate ahead of Kay and the twins. They wore riding breeches in case they might want to try the horses. After finding the precious stones, however, each was more interested in delving into the mansion's mysteries than going horseback riding.

"But none of us remembers where another red 'X' was," Wendy sighed.

"We can begin again on the spiral staircase," said Kay. "We haven't ripped up every step and perhaps we can find what Sara Cooke couldn't."

Kay borrowed Curran's tools and went to work.

"You are ruining these steps," Wendy disapproved.

"Never mind," panted Kay, prying away. "Maybe it will be worthwhile."

"I believe it is already," exclaimed Betty with a shout, as she seized something under the step. "It's a briefcase," she said, tugging at the article to get it from its dusty hiding place.

"What's in it?" questioned Wendy.

After some difficulty with the clasp, the girl opened the leather flap. Inside were various kinds of legal papers. There were patent rights to several inventions and a long white envelope securely sealed.

"What can be in that?" Betty asked with curiosity.

"I'd better wait for Bill to open it," said Kay.

"Then let's get home as fast as we can and find out," urged Betty eagerly. "We don't need to stay and compete with Chris's horsemanship!"

When the girls reached the law office, Bill looked up, surprised.

"Busy?" asked Kay apologetically.

"Busy at something you're interested in," he answered. "I've checked up on the nurse, Sara Cooke. She did take care of Greely and seems to be a thoroughly reliable person. I have just telephoned to her in New York and she is coming to Brantwood to tell what she knows about the late Manuel and his property."

"She said she had never been paid all her wages," Kay reminded him. "She was looking for the money due her when we saw her prying open the step."

"Funds from the estate are available now to pay her wages," said the attorney.

He was extremely interested in what the girls had brought. The contents of the sealed envelope proved to be stock in African gold mines.

As Bill put all the papers into his safe, Wendy said, "I guess the mansion almost did turn out to be a gold mine!"

"Have you heard any details about Peter's accident?" asked Betty.

"Not yet," the lawyer replied, "but I have been in touch with the authorities. As soon as facts are known I will get a cablegram from England and word also from Washington."

Saturday passed and another Sunday came and went in a jumble of unsolved secrets. Kay thought many times about the model Lamont. If he worked, why would he become a thief?

Distracted by the problem, Kay tumbled wearily into bed that night and dreamed crazily. Everything in the Greely case milled around in confusion in her mind!

She seemed to see Lester Lamont wearing a green dress suit and gardenias! He sat on the lawn with stuffed heads of wild beasts barking at him.

A large whale sat beside him, busily drawing architect's plans of the mansion. The man kept tugging at these plans and saying:

"Let me see, Grandfather!"

The whale very kindly showed him the sketches from time to time. From them Lamont made a model of the mansion with toy building blocks! Having finished his house, he again said:

"Let me see, Grandfather!"

The whale then took Chris's riding crop and pointed out red "X's" on his diagrams.

Lamont solemnly sprayed the red marks with perfume! He finally faded away and Kay woke up.

"O-o-o-h!" the girl moaned, opening her eyes and blinking in bewilderment. "What a terrible Alice-in-Wonderland feeling!"

This sensation remained with her all day. Just at

the close of school she had such a sudden inspiration that she nearly shouted aloud.

"I have a hunch, a wonderful hunch!" she said excitedly to herself. "That dream has solved one problem in the mystery, I believe!"

XXIV

A Forgotten Name

The moment school was over, Kay hurried away without waiting for Betty and Wendy. She wanted to test her idea alone.

She hurried off to interview an elderly woman who could remember when the Greely mansion was built. Kay felt sure that a key to the situation lay in the past and not in the present. She had to consult with someone old enough to know the past.

Such a person was Miss Esther Fulper, a withered little woman who had lived in Brantwood longer than anyone else could remember. She liked to write to the newspapers on various anniversaries, and usually called her articles "Reminiscences of Fifty Years Ago."

Miss Fulper was a sprightly, pleasant woman. She greeted Kay cordially and said she would be glad to tell all she knew about the mystery mansion.

"Yes, of course I remember when the Greely house was built," she replied to Kay's question. "There was a good deal of talk about it at the time. It was supposed to be very unusual."

"In what way?" asked Kay.

"Why, let me see. I believe there was something novel about the architect's plans. Folks said so in those days," said the woman reflectively.

"Do you know what these novel features were?" probed Kay.

"I can't remember offhand, but I could look through my diaries and clippings if it is important that you know," Miss Fulper offered.

"Do you remember any of the workmen or other people who might know about the way it was built?" Kay went on.

"The only ones I knew who were engaged in building the mansion were a carpenter and his son."

Kay's eyes brightened with hope.

"But both of them died long ago," said the old lady.

Kay's eyes darkened with disappointment. Was her questioning to be all in vain?

"Of course I knew the architect," Miss Fulper went on. "I remember him very well." She smiled reminiscently. "He used to be an old beau of mine."

Kay's hope of learning something about the mansion now returned.

"Do you recall anything about the plans he drew for the building?" the girl cross-questioned the woman.

"No, I wouldn't know anything about that," she said, "but I could tell you who it was he married. Her name was, let me see, Elsie, Elsie Something! What was her last name?"

Kay tried not to be impatient. "I don't need to know his wife's name," she interrupted, "but I would like to know about his novel designs for the unusual house."

"I told you that I didn't know that. It was some secret idea of Manny Greely's. John Vinson was the architect and John was not one to tell anybody's private business. I doubt if anyone knows a thing about the design of that house now."

"You say the architect's name was Vinson?" Kay asked. She recalled this name signed to the plans.

"John Vinson, yes. But it bothers me I can't think of the name of that girl he married. She was a plump blonde girl. Her father was an actor. I can see her as plain as day! She used to live over in Dunbar City. Now what was her last name?"

"It doesn't matter," Kay said gently.

"Well, anyway, they had one son, and he lived in Baltimore," said Miss Fulper, brightening and becoming definite in her recollections. "Then there was one grandson. A very handsome fellow he was."

She sat still without speaking for a few minutes. Suddenly she exclaimed, "I remember that girl's maiden name now!"

Kay repressed a sigh of impatience, but it quickly turned to a gasp of surprise.

"Lamont! That's what her name was! Elsie Lamont. Haven't thought of her in years!"

"Do you know where this Vinson grandson is?" asked Kay tensely.

"Lamont Vinson was in Baltimore the last I heard," replied Miss Fulper, "but of course he sometimes came up this way. Had relatives, I guess, in Dunbar City."

This was all the information that Kay could gather from the woman, but it was enough to work on. She hurried to Bill's office and greeted him with a broad grin.

"What makes you so happy?" he asked gloomily.

Things had not been going at all well with him that day. Kay's account of her interview quickly made him smile, however.

"How did you figure out that Lamont was Vinson's grandson and knew about the secrets of the mansion from knowledge of his grandfather's plans?"

"It was just a hunch," Kay laughed. "I had a dream. In the dream I saw Lamont asking his grandfather about the red 'X' marks on the plans. I've had an idea all along that the masked man had some good reason for stealing the set of plans. I figured he might have known about them."

"You're a terrific detective!" her cousin praised her.

"Please see if you can get any information on Lamont Vinson's present address," begged Kay.

The attorney called a lawyer friend of his in Baltimore. After a few remarks he put Kay on the phone.

"It just happens," said this Mr. Stone, "that I knew the Vinson family well. Fine people, except the grandson Lamont."

"Did he ever commit a crime?" asked Kay.

"No, not that," the lawyer replied. "But he was a spendthrift. In about five years he went through enough money for a frugal person to live on for fifty years."

"So now he may be hard up?" questioned the girl.

"He could be."

"Have you any idea what his address is or where he may be located now?" Kay inquired.

"No, I haven't," the attorney replied. "As a matter of fact, some friends of his told me the other day that no one around here had heard from him in some time."

Kay thanked Mr. Stone and hung up. She was both glad and disappointed at what she had heard. She was more sure than ever of the identity of the intruder at the Greely estate, but she was no nearer to locating him than she had been before.

Walking to the outer office, Kay was surprised to see the nurse, Sara Cooke. She was waiting to have an interview with Bill.

"Come right in," invited the lawyer.

The woman recognized Kay and referred to their conversation on the train.

"I didn't realize then that it would lead to anything, but your cousin tells me I may be able to help solve a mystery," she remarked.

To questions from the Traceys she replied that she had nursed Manuel Greely at the hospital in his last illness. She said he was delirious most of the time.

"I often heard him ramble on and on about secret hiding places in his house, and about an enormous fortune concealed here and there in nooks and crannies. I didn't take anything he raved about seriously," she said, "not even when he gave me a key and told me to get my salary from under the seventh step!

"When I did go, and found the step empty, I told myself it served me right for being so foolish. I ran away when I heard someone coming because I was ashamed of being caught in such a silly act. I was afraid it would look as if I were trying to steal! Of course," said Sara Cooke proudly, "that is really the last thing I ever would do!"

"I am sure it is," said Bill Tracey with conviction.

"Do you happen to recall any other places mentioned by Mr. Greely as holding treasure?" asked Kay.

"Well—" The woman hesitated. "I didn't pay much attention, but I think he mentioned that he kept personal things in a chest under a hearthstone in one of the rooms."

Kay and her relative exchanged quick glances at this piece of information.

"He said he kept his family Bible in this chest, with his family tree and records, and other valuable papers."

"Did he mention a will?" Bill asked quickly.

"That's important, because we think he died without one. None has been found."

"I don't recall that he did," the woman replied slowly. "Come to think of it, he did say something about a special paper."

"I expect we'll find it in that box if we can locate the box," said the lawyer.

"Probably the chest was stolen!" groaned Kay. "We found a hearthstone half pulled out," she explained, "and a man running away with a box under his arm."

Just then the buzzer sounded. There was a telephone call for Kay.

"Oh, yes, Miss Fulper," the girl replied. "What is that you say?"

"I said, John Vinson's grandson has just called on me!" squeaked the old lady's cracked voice at the other end of the line.

"What did he want?" asked Kay, her voice shrill with excitement.

"He says he has information of value to the heirs of Manuel Greely, and he wanted to know if I knew who they are and how to get in touch with them."

"Is he there now?" asked Kay excitedly.

"No, I told him to come back in an hour and in the meantime I'd try to get the address he wants. I thought that would give you a chance to get here and interview him if you want to."

"That's quick thinking!" cried Kay. "My cousin, who is the lawyer for the Greely estate, will come over with me at once! Entertain Mr. La—Mr. Vinson and try to keep him there until we can get to your house!"

Excusing themselves from Sara Cooke, the girl and her cousin got a plainclothesman and drove rapidly to Miss Fulper's residence. Upon their arrival they saw her on her front porch frantically beckoning.

"He's gone!" she cried. "I couldn't persuade him to wait! He left here in a black car."

"Which way did he go?" demanded Bill.

"Straight out toward the Greely estate."

Bill immediately turned his car in that direction.

"He's up to something again," growled the lawyer.

No time was lost in covering the ground between Brantwood and the gray mansion. The Tracey car raced up Hemlock Lane and skidded to a stop at the front door. A terrific commotion was going on inside the house.

Kay peered in a window. The sight within startled her!

XXV

Good Fortune

Kay, gazing through the window, saw Mulligan and Curran in a wild struggle. Both were grappling with a man who fought like a wildcat! He was quick and athletic, and more sprightly than either of the two older men.

She caught a glimpse of his face from which Curran had ripped a mask. It was the same intruder!

Battling wildly, his clothes torn and his lip bleeding, the prisoner wrenched himself free and plunged desperately toward the door. Kay had just darted to the entrance as the escaping thief flung himself through it. They collided violently.

Instantly Mulligan and Curran hurled themselves upon the man. Bill joined the fight and pinned down the man's arms while the plainclothesman snapped handcuffs on his wrists.

"Don't take him to the police station until we find out some details from him," Bill instructed, as the detective took charge.

"Your name is Vinson, isn't it?" the lawyer began sternly.

The dishevelled captive looked surprised but would not reply.

"Lamont is the name you've been using around here" was Bill's next comment.

"That was your grandmother's maiden name!" Kay spoke up.

The man looked astonished that the Traceys had this personal information. Still he refused to speak.

"You are a model," said the lawyer, "but also you are the grandson of the architect of this house."

"You used a mask as a disguise because you were afraid your face might be recognized from your pictures in dog food, perfume, and other advertisements. Isn't that so?" Kay asked.

"Yes, that's true!" admitted the culprit. "I'm Lamont Vinson," he owned up sullenly. "I guess you know too much for me to deny it."

"Why didn't you use your own name around here?" asked Bill.

"Because Lester Lamont sounded better professionally," the man explained.

"Where are the things you stole from the Greely house?" Bill demanded.

"What business is that of yours?" retorted Lamont sourly. "You aren't the Greely heirs!"

"I have been employed as the attorney to settle the Greely estate," Bill explained. "You thought any heir there might be didn't know there was fortune in the house and might pay you for telling about it, didn't you?" continued the lawyer.

"That's right," Vinson said glumly.

"You'll return everything you stole or go to jail, mister!" the policeman interrupted harshly.

"Don't send me to jail!" protested the captive. "I can't bring disgrace on my father's name!"

"This is a bad time to think about that. We'll judge the case later," said Bill. "How did you know about the mansion containing secret hiding places?"

"I used to hear my grandfather tell about it, and the idea intrigued me ever since I was a child," the prisoner explained. "He used to amuse me with stories about secret compartments he had built, and also secret entrances and exits. I always wanted to see this place. When I needed money I thought I might sell the information to someone," he confessed. "I didn't steal anything for myself," he emphasized.

"You stole the plans," Kay spoke up.

"I found them. I don't call it stealing to pick up some old papers from the floor of a vacant house— papers that belonged to my grandfather and had his name signed to them. I used them to help the heir locate his own property. He might have lost it if I hadn't. You can't put me in jail for that!"

This cross-examination was suddenly interrupted by the appearance of the big police dog. It stalked out of the woods and ambled toward the house looking for its master. Between its teeth the animal clutched a roll of papers.

"There's your dog!" said Kay. "What's in its mouth?"

"Gray is trained to carry rolled-up newspapers and packages for me," said Vinson. "I don't know what he has now."

The dog had trotted directly to its master and now stood in the doorway.

"It has those architect's plans!" gasped Kay.

"Here, Gray," called Lamont. "Good dog, drop 'em!"

Gray looked suspiciously at the other people present and refused to obey. A deep growl rumbled in its throat.

"My dog has been taught to retrieve whatever I drop and fetch it to me," explained the prisoner. "I dropped those plans in my hurry and Gray found them. He won't give them to anyone but me. You better take off these handcuffs and let me manage him."

"Oh, no, smart boy!" replied the policeman. "That's a good scheme to get loose but you can't fool us so easily. You sit still and keep your bracelets on and we'll manage your dog."

The beast growled and refused to give up its prize. No threat or coaxing, even from Lamont himself, availed. Finally Kay ran to the kitchen and returned with a plate of meat.

"My dinner!" lamented Curran.

"Never mind!" said Kay, tossing a juicy piece of steak to the dog. The animal sniffed, hesitated, then dropped the plans and stepped forward to gulp down the bait. Kay threw out another tempting morsel. While the animal was eating it, Curran rescued the roll of papers.

The big dog licked its chops, whirled about, and jumped to recover the plans. The watchman, clutching them, dashed up the stairway for safety. The dog, disregarding its master's command, pursued Curran and might have bitten him, but help arrived just in time. Cody entered the house at that moment wearing a full cowboy outfit.

Gray's bared teeth were threatening Tom's leg, when there was the hiss of a lariat uncoiling in mid-air! The lasso snapped out like a rattlesnake striking! Its slip noose settled about the dog's throat and jerked tight, choking the animal.

"I've got you now!" said Cody triumphantly as he dragged the animal away and tied it fast. He then turned on Lamont angrily. "You stole my horse!" he charged.

"I only borrowed him!" the other man countered. "Your mount threw me and ran away or I would have returned him!"

"Well, I've borrowed your dog now, and I don't intend to give him back in a hurry, I can tell you that!"

retorted the ranchman. "He's a menace and a public nuisance!"

The Traceys were delighted that the model and his pet had been captured. Both were public nuisances.

As the prisoner seemed entirely cowed, Kay ventured to ask, "You found a chest of important papers under a hearthstone, didn't you?"

"Yes," Vinson admitted.

"There was a will among them, wasn't there?" the lawyer guessed.

The Traceys hung on the answer.

"Yes, there was," the man said slowly. "The whole Greely estate was left to a grandnephew named Peter."

His listeners, although not surprised at this announcement, felt pangs of sorrow. They gave no outward sign of being disturbed, however. Bill Tracey merely said in a professional tone:

"This clears up a good many things. Now we'll go back to town."

Vinson, handcuffed and closely guarded by the policeman, occupied the rear seat of the Tracey car on the ride into Brantwood. Kay sat in front with her cousin, who drove. Leaving their passengers at the courthouse, the Traceys went their way.

"I have to stop at my office," said the lawyer.

"I'll come, too," replied Kay. "I want to call Mother."

The Traceys, entering the suite, were talking together so busily that at first they did not notice a man who rose to meet them. Even when he spoke, neither of them recognized him. Suddenly Kay shouted:

"*Peter Greely!* Where did you come from?"

"Out of the air!" replied the young pilot cheerily.

"You were reported—the newspapers said—" Kay gasped.

Peter laughed. "The accounts were exaggerated.

My plane was only slightly damaged. I came home by clipper."

"This is wonderful!" cried Kay, shaking one of his hands while Bill grasped the other.

"You are just in time to help straighten out your estate," his lawyer announced. "Do you realize, Mr. Greely, that you are a millionaire?"

At this astonishing news the young man dropped into the nearest chair! A few days later he and Bill Tracey managed to get his affairs fairly well settled. The stolen chest, secured from Vinson with other belongings, contained many helpful papers. The treasures located by Kay and the twins were appraised and found to be of immense value.

"Miss Tracey," said Peter to Kay, "I have been magically transformed from a poor man to a rich one by your quick-wittedness as a detective."

Kay laughed.

"But seriously," Peter said, "I want to reward you. I've heard about your unhappy experience at the perfume factory and your wish to restore the loss. The least I can do is to give you some of the ambergris you found. The rest can go to Mulligan. I think your friends, Betty and Wendy, and also Ronald Earle should be given something for their help also."

"You're much too generous. How can we ever thank you?" said Kay, deeply moved.

"I am the one to thank *you!*" insisted Peter.

"The thing we are most grateful for is your safe return!" declared Kay earnestly. "Carmont High School would like you to give us a talk on what it feels like to fly over the Atlantic Ocean and make a safe landing in a crippled plane!"

The students were very excited on the day the pilot gave his lively speech. Chris Eaton, watching Kay and her friends chatting and laughing with Peter Greely, was consumed by envy. She tried her very best to find out what had been discovered in his mansion but she was unsuccessful.

The Worth twins, Ronald Earle, and Kay Tracey too, all kept silent about it.

The mysteries of the mansion of secrets were to remain a deep, dark secret to the outside world!

KAY TRACEY®
MYSTERIES

Kay Tracey—an amateur detective so sharp that even the best professional might envy her skills. You'll want to follow all these suspense-filled adventures of Kay and her friends.

By Frances K. Judd

15080	**THE DOUBLE DISGUISE #1**	**$1.75**
15081	**IN THE SUNKEN GARDEN #2**	**$1.75**
15082	**THE SIX FINGERED GLOVE MYSTERY #3**	**$1.75**
15070	**THE MANSION OF SECRETS #4**	**$1.75**
15071	**THE GREEN CAMEO MYSTERY #5**	**$1.75**
15072	**THE MESSAGE IN THE SAND DUNES #6**	**$1.75**

Buy them at your local bookstore or use this handy coupon for ordering: